FOUND: HIS FAMILY

FOUND: HIS FAMILY

BY

NICOLA MARSH

MILLS & BOON®

First published in Great Britain 2006
Large Print edition 2006
Harlequin Mills & Boon Limited,
Eton House, 18-24 Paradise Road,
Richmond, Surrey TW9 1SR

© Nicola Marsh 2006

ISBN-13: 978 0 263 19027 4
ISBN-10:   0 263 19027 7

Set in Times Roman 17 on 21½ pt.
16-1206-46136

Printed and bound in Great Britain
by Antony Rowe Ltd, Chippenham, Wiltshire

Special thanks to two people who helped make this book happen: Ola, for her medical input, and my editor, Emily, for her enthusiasm and patience.

CHAPTER ONE

AIMEE PAYET loved chocolate.

She loved savouring the melt-in-your-mouth texture on her tongue, drinking its delicious sweetness and kneading the sticky bits of heaven with her nimble fingers as she produced yet another masterpiece for Payet's Patisserie, the cake shop she'd successfully managed for the last two years since her parents' death.

Today, however, even chocolate couldn't ease the deep sense of impending doom that hung over her like a storm cloud about to dump its deluge in a catastrophic downpour.

She glanced at her watch, the same action she'd done every few minutes for the last hour, her stomach churning as closing time grew nearer. Jed had left a message saying he'd be here at six, and if he hadn't changed since she'd last seen him, he'd be here on the dot.

And her world would come crashing down around her.

'Aimee?'

The moment he said her name, the last five years rolled away, his deep voice washing over her in a familiarity which took her breath away.

It wasn't supposed to be like this. She'd dealt with her feelings, moved on, created a life for her and Toby. A life that didn't included Jed Sanderson, her first love, her *past* love. A life where they didn't need him. Until now.

Pasting a forced smile on her face while her insides churned with dread at what she had to tell him, she turned to face him. 'Hi, Jed. Thanks for coming.'

The words sounded small, soft, as if she were hearing them through the wall of thick fog that occasionally rolled off Port Phillip Bay and shrouded Melbourne in its pea-soup density.

'Are you all right?'

No, she wanted to scream. *Nothing's all right and, after I tell you the truth, nothing ever will be again.*

Focusing her attention with effort, she saw the concern in his light brown eyes.

Eyes the colour of warm caramel.

Eyes that had captivated her from the first minute she'd seen them all those years ago.

Eyes that would soon fill with anger and pain when she told him about Toby. And what she wanted from him.

'I've been better,' she finally admitted, fiddling with the cash register, dropping her gaze to her fingernails, which were chewed to the quick courtesy of the earth-shattering news she'd received about Toby two days ago.

'Look, why don't you sit down and I'll get you a drink?'

Before she could blink, he had scouted around the counter, taken gentle hold of her arm and was leading her to a corner table.

'You don't understand…' she started to say,

shrugging off his hold while biting down on her lower lip to stop herself from crying. 'I need to close up before we talk.'

'Let me.'

He strode to the door, flipped the sign to 'closed' and turned the lock. The soft clunk of metal on metal resounded in her head as she suddenly realised her predicament: she was locked in her shop with Jed, the guy who'd broken her heart. The guy she'd never wanted to see again as long as she lived. The guy who'd fathered her son.

People streamed past the floor-to-ceiling glass windows as they bustled along Acland Street, St Kilda's busiest thoroughfare any time of day or night, and she stared at them in anger, wishing she could be like them, without a care in the world. Jed had been her past and now, thanks to a cruel twist of fate, he could become her present.

'I was surprised to hear from you after all this time,' he said, leaning against the counter and looking way too handsome in his pinstripe designer suit, pale green shirt and matching tie, his dark hair curling around his collar the way it used to. 'An Express Post letter seemed a bit formal. You could've called if it was that urgent.'

No, she couldn't. Holding herself together following the doctor's appointment had been hard enough without hearing Jed's voice, hearing the judgement and censure when she told him the truth, a truth that would blow him away.

'No, I needed to see you. The phone wouldn't cut it for this.'

'I'm intrigued.'

He smiled, a simple action which illuminated his eyes with warmth. Similar to the reaction his light grip had on her as he guided her to the table, infusing her with a reassuring heat she hadn't felt since she'd last hugged her dad.

Dad...Mum...I wish you were here. I need you so much; Toby needs you so much.

How many times had she sent this silent plea heavenward over the last two years since her parents had unexpectedly died in a freak storm? Too many times to count and, once again, it went unheralded.

If her parents were around, she wouldn't be about to have this conversation with a man she'd never intended to see again. They could've been tested as donors, the odds in favour that one of them would've been compatible and everything would've been OK.

Instead she'd been forced to contact Jed out of sheer desperation and, now he was here, she still had no idea if he would help her. She'd thought she'd known him inside and out at one stage.

She'd been wrong.

'Before you pass out on me, how about I get you a coffee? Then we can have this talk that's making you look like you've got a story and a half to tell me.'

She shook her head, finding the experience of being waited on by Jed in her own shop strangely surreal.

'If anyone needs a hit of caffeine, you do,' he

said, his astute gaze sweeping over her as if he expected her to faint at his feet any second.

'That would be great,' she said, too tired to resist, too worried to argue.

Besides, he was right. She needed a jolt to jumpstart her brain, which had partially shut down since she'd seen the doctor and he'd delivered his mind-numbing news in a soul-destroying, terrifying week.

'Mind if I have one? I could use a caffeine boost myself.'

'Of course! I'm sorry, my mind is elsewhere.'

'Don't apologise. Flat white OK?'

She nodded and watched him handle the espresso machine like a pro. Dressed like that, she could imagine him with an army of subordinates serving him any type of coffee he chose any time of the day yet here he was, looking at home in the cosy space behind the counter of Payet's Patisserie. Surreal didn't come close to describing this bizarre encounter and it was about to get worse. A whole lot worse.

'Help yourself to any cake you like,' she said, knowing she should get up and do it herself but finding the lethargy that had invaded her body the last few days had spread now that she'd finally sat down.

Stopping wasn't a good thing. Keeping busy was the key. The key to coping. To not focusing on the past. To not thinking about the future. It was how she'd survived the last few days, how she'd struggled to mend her broken heart after leaving Jed, how she'd raised Toby, how she'd always been the strong one in her family.

A family which had been decimated by tragedy, a family now consisting of Toby and her. And Jed, if he came through for them.

Yet right now, as strong as she tried to be, it felt good to let someone else take charge for a change, even if that someone was the last man on earth she would've approached, given a choice.

'Thanks, but I'm watching my weight.'

He patted his waistline after placing two steaming coffees in front of them and smiled, a small, self-deprecating smile, and for the first time since Toby's diagnosis she found herself responding.

The slight upturning of her lips at the corners felt foreign, like muscles stretching after the first Pilates class she'd ever taken, yet it felt good at the same time. Who would've thought Jed could actually make her smile again after what they'd been through, what they'd said to each other at the end?

However, her smile vanished as quickly as it had come. What was she thinking? Toby was dying and she was wasting time trading smiles with Jed. She needed to get on with things, with convincing him to help. Her momentary lapse had to be anxiety, a purely nervous reaction to a life-threatening situation and the role Jed would play. She hoped.

'Ready to talk?'

Nodding, she took a quick gulp of coffee which scalded her tongue. Good, it might take the edge off her urge to bawl on his broad shoulders.

'Whatever it is, it must be pretty bad for you to approach me after all this time.'

Cradling the hot mug in her hand, she peered at him over the rim, liking the changes the years had wrought. The smattering of grey in his black hair, the fine lines radiating from the corners of his striking eyes adding a seriousness to the boyish face which had once charmed her into loving him.

Though she'd dated through uni and been serious with one guy for about eight months, the minute she'd set foot on Dunk Island, walked into the restaurant for her first real job since graduating top of her French-pastry class and spied Jed she'd fallen. Hard.

They'd created magic together before her dreams deflated like a saggy soufflé.

Banishing her useless memories, she said, 'I need your help.'

She had to keep it simple, short, straightforward. Lay the facts out before him, state her case, appeal to his better side, the side she knew he had despite how he'd pushed her away all those years ago.

'With what?' He paused, fixing her with the soul-searching stare only he did so well, his confident grin grating on her thinly stretched nerves. 'You know I'm a supportive kind of guy.'

'Yeah, right. Like the way you supported me right out of our relationship?'

Where had that come from? Why did she sound so accusatory, so annoyed, as though she still cared?

Shutters descended over his eyes in an instant, blocking out the warmth, shutting her out as he always had when he didn't want to give her answers.

'You wanted something I couldn't give you back then.'

'Couldn't or wouldn't?'

'It's not important.' His lips set in a thin, stubborn line just the way they had used to and the familiar action ignited an old grudge that had been simmering for a few years.

'Not important? I guess you would see it like that.'

He shook his head, anger tightening his features into hard angles. 'Is this why you dragged me to Melbourne? To beat me up over something that happened five years ago? That *finished* five years ago?'

'No, there's something else.'

Suddenly she deflated, annoyed that she'd let him get to her like that. What had happened between them was over and had been for a long time. She'd dealt with it; she'd moved on. Why dredge up the past when it would only be detrimental to her cause? She needed to get him onside, not offensive.

'Tell me.'

Swallowing the painful lump lodged in her throat, she raised her eyes to his, seeing a wary curiosity there as if he half expected another verbal spray.

'My son's ill,' she blurted, blinking back tears at the injustice.

If anyone had to get sick, why couldn't it be her? She was strong; she could handle it. She'd handled losing Jed, losing her parents. She was tough; she could take it. But Toby...he had his whole life in front of him. Her precious little boy had just turned five, would start school soon, had enrolled in a little athletics pro-gramme and had a zest for life that left her breathless and laughing most days.

Though the minute he'd turned lethargic, pale, with unexplained ugly bruises on his spindly arms and legs, she'd known. Something was dreadfully wrong and a visit to the doctor and a few blood tests had confirmed it.

Acute lymphoblastic leukaemia. The kind of disease that killed, the kind of disease her cheeky, gorgeous boy had no right contracting.

'You have a son?' A dark eyebrow shot up, lending him a weirdly comical look when there was nothing remotely funny about their situation.

Your son, she needed to say but instead she took another gulp of coffee, postponing the inevitable for another few seconds while furiously marshalling her thoughts.

How should she tell him? Straight out or work up to it? She'd mentally rehearsed this speech a hundred times in her head since he'd responded to her urgent plea, yet now her mouth couldn't form the words.

'He's a lovely little boy.' *Tall like you, and those soft brown eyes exactly like yours.* 'He's just been diagnosed with leukaemia.' She waved her hand around in a vague gesture, wondering if he'd get it.

By the compassionate expression on his handsome face, he did.

'I'm sorry. How awful for you.'

He reached towards her as if to place his hand over hers and she scuttled back like a scared mouse, her earlier misgivings about being locked up with him resurfacing. If seeing him again had packed a power-punch, having him touch her to offer comfort had the potential to undo her completely.

He didn't say a word though she saw surprise flicker in the depths of his eyes and regret stabbed her at how far apart they'd grown. They'd been the invincible couple, the couple that everyone made gagging sounds about over their mushiness, the couple that couldn't keep their hands off each other. They were the forever couple.

But, as she'd found out the hard way, nothing lasted forever.

Taking a deep breath, she launched down the path of no return. 'Toby needs a bone-marrow transplant and I'm not compatible.'

'Hell.' He ran a hand through his hair, sending dark spikes shooting in every direction. 'You need my help? Is it money? Do you need to start a donor search? Fund-raising? I can get the TV station to help. I can—'

'I need you to be tested.'

There, she'd said it, though her voice came out on a soft squeak that had Jed sitting forward to hear it.

'Me? But I'm not family…' He trailed off, a flicker of comprehension flashing across his face in a microsecond before he continued in a cold, dull monotone. 'How old is Toby?'

'Five.'

She tilted her head up, meeting his dazed stare directly, not ashamed of the choices she'd made.

If Jed hadn't wanted marriage back then, how would he have handled fatherhood? Dads were reliable, stable, rock-like types you could depend on, the type of amazing, supportive man she'd been lucky enough to have for a dad, not guys who couldn't come clean to their girl-friends let alone enter a life-long commitment.

Whichever way she looked at it, she'd made the right choice in not telling Jed when she'd discovered her pregnancy. He'd moved on and so had she. He'd become Australia's sexiest TV chef; she had a successful career, a booming business and a son she wouldn't trade for all the tortes in Vienna. Toby was happy.

She was happy. And then God had had to go and pull the rug out from under them.

'Five.' He repeated the number in a flat drone as if not quite comprehending the maths. 'But that would mean—'

'He's yours.'

She sagged back against the seat, wrapping her arms around her middle in a purely protective gesture against the warring emotions flashing across Jed's expressive face.

Disbelief, shock and confusion turned his eyes to molten caramel while he flushed beneath his tan.

'*What?*'

'Toby is your son,' she repeated, finally giving in to the tears that had threatened since the minute she'd laid eyes on Jed again.

'My son,' he said softly, as if trying the words on for size, before the anger she'd been expecting erupted to the surface in a hot, fierce explosion. 'My *son*? What the hell is going on here?'

CHAPTER TWO

JED watched Aimee, his gaze never leaving her face for a second. Any moment now she'd yell 'fooled you' and laugh, the same, bubbly laugh he'd loved years ago, the laugh that chased all his troubles away. Back then, he'd had a few.

'Look, I know it's a shock to you and believe me, I wouldn't have involved you if I hadn't been desperate, but—'

'Stop it! Just stop right there.'

He stood up so quickly his chair toppled over, hitting the black and white tiled floor with a loud thud, and he resisted the urge to kick it.

Not only had the woman he'd once loved more than life itself just announced he was a father, but she also had to rub it in that he was the last person she'd approach unless desperate.

A father.

He closed his eyes, the two words echoing through his head like an old vinyl record stuck on replay.

How could he be a father when he didn't know how? When it could only lead to disaster?

He'd tried the role once before in raising Bud and look how that had turned out. No way, fatherhood wasn't for him. Some guys just weren't cut out for that whole responsibility thing and he was one of them.

'Jed, I know this is hard for you but please, try to put your own feelings on hold for a second and think of Toby.'

He opened his eyes and stared at the woman who had lied to him for the last five years, a woman who, for one crazy second when he'd read her urgent summons, he'd hoped might still feel something for him. What a joke. Unfortunately, he didn't feel like laughing in this whole bizarre scenario.

'Don't you dare talk to me about feelings because frankly, you haven't got a clue.'

'You're angry,' she said, her hazel eyes filled with an understanding which had him wanting to punch a hole in the nearest wall.

He didn't want her understanding. He wanted answers, starting with why she'd deprived him of the chance to know he had a son.

'Damn right I'm angry.'

He righted the chair and slid into it, running a hand over his face as if to erase the last few minutes. 'Actually, angry doesn't come close to how I'm feeling. My God, what were you thinking, keeping something like this from me?'

She blanched and raised stricken eyes to his. 'Would it have made a difference?'

'A difference to what? To us?'

Her mute nod sent blonde curls cascading forward, effectively shading her face but not before he'd seen the sheen of tears.

Damn it, he hated tears. They made him feel helpless, and right now he didn't want to feel anything other than anger towards her. She didn't deserve his compassion. She didn't deserve the intense, almost visceral impulse to bundle her into his arms and comfort her.

Suddenly, it dawned on him and his fury ignited anew.

'Is that what all that marriage talk was about? You knew you were pregnant before we broke up and didn't tell me?'

'Of course not!' A faint pink put some colour back in her pale cheeks, accentuating the gold flecks in her eyes, those same flecks that had used to glow with emotion, with passion.

'Then when? When did you find out?'

Her hand crept up to her mouth, the nervous gesture annoying him when years ago he'd found it endearing.

'After we'd broken up. I'd already returned to Melbourne and started work here when I realised.'

'Realised what? Realised you were about to bring a child into this world without a father?

Realised you made a decision that affected the both of us without consulting me?'

'But it didn't affect you. You weren't around. You were never going to be around!'

Her chest heaved, her eyes flashed and she slammed her hand onto the table, rattling the cups in their saucers. 'You have no right to question my decision. You had the opportunity to build a future with me, to have the life we'd always talked about, but you bailed out. You! Not me. Why would I take the risk on you bailing out on my son as well?'

'Our son,' he automatically corrected and blinked in surprise, her accusations sitting like a heavy stone on his heart.

She was right. He had walked away from the best thing to ever happen to him though not by choice. He'd had to push her away, to save her from the scandal that would've ripped their relationship apart.

He'd made his decision at the time, the only choice available to him, yet here he was, questioning her choices? Giving her a hard time when they had more important things to think about, like saving the boy's life?

'This isn't getting us anywhere,' he said, swallowing his bitterness at the unfairness of it all. 'Tell me more about Toby.'

The tension drained from her body and she slumped into her seat again, the harried expression slipping over her face like a well-worn mask. 'You're sure you can handle this?'

Hell, what kind of man did she think he was? The useless, spineless, weak man his father had been? No, he was nothing like dear old Dad, the man who had cost him a future with the woman staring at him as if he could morph into a monster at any second.

'What do you want me to handle? My instant fatherhood? That Toby is sick? Or the fact that you lied to me and I'll never be able to forgive you for it?'

Hurt flickered in her eyes, a flash of unadulterated pain that made him feel guilty, though it didn't last. His emotions were too raw, too intense, too devastating for him to give her an inch.

She saw him as some last-ditch option, as a man not worthy of knowing he had a son unless it was a matter of life and death, and the truth hurt like hell, making him want to lash out in return.

'I don't want your forgiveness, I want your help,' she said, her defiance startling when he almost expected her to fall apart if her pale face and bloodshot eyes were any indication.

Not that he wanted her to. He didn't want to play knight in shining armour, not when he had more pressing matters like trying to assimilate the fact he was a father.

'That's right, you're desperate,' he sneered, pushing away from the table and striding to the window, hating himself for pushing her like this but unable to stop. A deep, perverse need to punish her egged him on, to make her pay for keeping him in the dark because she hadn't trusted him enough.

'I'm sorry.' Her soft touch on his arm made him jump and he jerked away, needing distance between them before he did something even more out of character, such as walk out the door and never look back.

Though to Aimee's way of thinking, that wouldn't be so unexpected. For all he knew, she probably expected him to run. Again.

Staring blindly out the window, he saw a guy with a stroller unbuckle a little boy from the contraption, swing and settle him on top of his shoulders, both grinning madly as they trotted off down the street. He'd seen kids and dads a thousand times before and the scene had never affected him the way it did at that moment, a hard, tight knot forming in the pit of his stomach, making him feel sick that he had a little boy of his own and knew nothing about him. That he'd never be any good at any of that father-son stuff that was expected of dads.

Though Aimee wasn't asking him to be a father to Toby. She only wanted him to get tested as a donor. Somehow, that made him feel a whole lot worse.

Ignoring the churning dread in his gut, he turned to face her. 'I can deal with the anger stuff. Right now, tell me what I need to do about Toby.'

Her gaze searched his face for a moment, apparently satisfied by what she saw. 'OK. We don't have much time so I took the liberty of making an appointment with the doctor tonight for you to get tested and ask any questions you might have.'

Her presumptuousness—her assumption that he'd drop everything and help her after the way things had ended between them—rankled like nothing else.

He needed more time. Time to come to grips with the bomb she'd just dropped on him, time to grasp the full reality of what being a dad meant, time to gain control over the slow-burning anger that made him want to explode all over again.

However, three little words penetrated his dazed brain. *Not much time…*

Aimee had approached him out of desperation and the little guy didn't have much time.

He couldn't wallow in his anger or stew over her deception, he had to make a choice. Now. And just like five years earlier, it was a no-brainer.

'Fine. I'll do it. When do I get to meet Toby?'

She averted her gaze, staring out the window behind him. 'It will be too late tonight so it'll have to be tomorrow. He's so tired all the time and the hospital keep pretty strict visiting hours.'

'Even for parents?'

'N-no, parents are welcome any time.'

Her slight hesitation had him on full alert. She was hiding something. Something else, and suddenly it hit him like an exploding volcano: swift, scorching, devastating, and burning an agonising trail right through his soul.

She didn't want him to meet Toby.

If he had the test and wasn't compatible, she wanted him to walk away. To leave as if nothing had changed, as if his son didn't exist.

Well, he had news for her.

'I know you don't see me as father material but I'm here now and I'd like a chance to meet my son.'

The words fell out of his mouth in a rush, as if by saying them he couldn't take them back. And right then, it hit him. He didn't want to take them back, despite the fear he'd be lousy father material.

My son.

He still couldn't comprehend the two words and had no idea how he really felt or what he'd say when he came face to face with Toby, but suddenly he was damn sure about one thing. He wanted a chance, a chance to meet his son.

Aimee nodded, her shoulders slumped in weary defeat as if she'd gone ten rounds with him and lost. 'You ready to go to the hospital now? It's not far.'

'Let's go.' He tried to inject some life into his voice but it fell flat as he mulled over the truth he'd just learned and the implications for them all.

Aimee moved around the shop like an automaton, flicking off lights, pulling down blinds and setting the coolers for the cakes. His protective instincts urged him to help her but he didn't move, sensing she needed to do the simple, repetitive actions as a way to buy time to steady her emotions.

If she was feeling half as punch-drunk as he was after their confrontation, she'd be an emotional wreck on the inside.

Besides, she didn't need his help. She'd made it clear that she'd been doing fine on her own without him these last five years and it stuck in his craw, fuelling his latent resentment that she viewed him as some sort of stopgap measure.

'Jed?'

He jumped, surprised by the quiver in her voice as she snuck up behind him.

'Yeah?'

'Thanks for doing this. For being here with me.' Tears shimmered in her eyes as she looked up at him, as if beseeching him to understand. 'For being here for Toby.'

He was angry, shaken, confused, yet when she finally gave into the tears that had been threatening he had no option but to envelop her in his arms, smooth her hair and make soft, soothing noises as his anger shifted slightly to be replaced by an emotion he didn't want to acknowledge, an emotion that had fuelled his actions years earlier, an emotion that could only lead to more pain.

Guilt could be a terrible thing.

CHAPTER THREE

JED stared at the doctor's lips, watching them move, hearing the words but having trouble processing them.

Acute lymphoblastic leukaemia.

The diagnosis sounded so much worse coming from the uptight medic in a too-tight white coat, the word 'leukaemia' reverberating around Jed's head till he wanted to run from the room, find a secluded corner and curl up in a tight ball with his hands over his ears.

He'd had a similar gut-wrenching reaction when the head juror had pronounced his father guilty, and later when the judge had sentenced him to ten years behind bars.

'You sure about this?'

He met the doctor's disapproving gaze that

read 'how dare you question me?' straight on,
praying this *was* a mistake, that the doc would
clear his throat, apologise and send them on
their way with a prescription for antibiotics.

However, he'd given up on prayers being
answered around the time his dad had done his
first stint in jail and he knew without a doubt
that his current plea to God was just as futile.

The doctor shook his head, his fingers toying
with a fancy gold pen as he reinforced the news
that sent a chill down his spine.

'I'm sorry. We ran extensive tests and they
were conclusive. Toby's loss of appetite,
fatigue, frequent nose bleeds and bruising had
me concerned when Aimee first brought him in
and I had a fair idea what we'd find.'

'I see,' Jed said, not seeing in the slightest,
questioning the injustice of a world where the
bad guys usually won and a helpless little boy
had to cope with an illness like this.

'What's the treatment?' To his credit, his

voice remained steady while his insides roiled in one huge, anxious mess.

The doctor continued to fiddle with his pen, rolling it over and over with his fingers, and he had the sudden urge to lean over and slam his hand on top of it.

'There are several components to treatment,' the doctor said, his cool detachment annoying him almost as much as his fiddling fingers. 'Toby has a good prognosis as his white blood-cell count is less than thirty thousand, and with chemotherapy and radiation therapy his chances of remission are high.'

Chemotherapy…radiation therapy…remission…

The words echoed through his head, banging and crashing their way through the neurons and triggering a blinding headache that left him paralysed.

Toby didn't deserve this. Nobody deserved this. He'd seen the suffering on TV and in the newspapers, seen kids with pale faces, bald heads and brave smiles. His heart had gone out to them and now the son he'd only just discovered would go through the same torture all in the name of survival.

'Of course, a bone-marrow transplant gives the best hope for not having a relapse.'

'Is a transplant always necessary?' Jed asked, bracing himself for the next bombshell this cruel man dropped. Though in all fairness, it wasn't the doc's fault. He was here to help them, and from now on they'd be placing a lot of faith in his skills. If only he'd stop tapping that damn pen on the file in front of him!

'Not always. Some people are cured after just chemical intervention. However, it's best to consider all possibilities.' The doctor tilted his head forward and stared at him over the top of his steel-rimmed spectacles as if willing him to comprehend what he was telling him.

Damn, this wasn't fair. The diagnosis, the fact Aimee hadn't told him about Toby before this, the chance to be a dad to Toby ripped from him before he could try, even if he sucked at it.

In the midst of his self-pity, it struck him. Aimee had already gone through this, had heard the diagnosis, the treatment, the chances. Alone.

She'd gone through this horrible experience by herself, and suddenly the guilt returned. Guilt at how he'd treated her, how he hadn't been around, how he'd never known his son and might not have that chance now. He needed to get over it and move on, for all their sakes.

'Tell Jed about the transplant,' Aimee said, a hint of steel threaded through the softness of her voice, and his admiration for her skyrocketed.

The doctor nodded. 'An allogenic bone-marrow transplant usually comes from a sibling donor, from a relative or even a compatible stranger. We harvest the bone marrow, which is the liquid centre of bone, from the donor and the recipient gets it in an IV over one to five hours.'

'IV? Oh.' Jed winced, hoping his son didn't

have his phobia for needles. 'What does the harvesting procedure involve?'

Though he had a sneaking suspicion he knew. His high-school biology wasn't that rusty and he remembered covering BMT—bone-marrow transplants—in an assignment.

The doctor's pen tapping increased as if he didn't have time for such mundane questions and Jed briefly envisioned ramming that pen in a few places a pen shouldn't be.

'The donor is given an anaesthetic, a needle is inserted into the hip bone and the marrow drawn out. Harvesting the marrow takes about an hour and is more uncomfortable for the donor than the recipient.'

'Great. About time you gave me some good news,' Jed muttered, his sarcasm not lost on the doctor, who actually looked as if he might crack a smile for all of two seconds.

'Anything else you'd like to ask?' The doctor paused for a moment before rushing on, obviously none too keen on further questions. 'If not, I'd like to have you tested as soon as possible.'

'Just one more thing.'

All this medical talk of various treatment methods was fine but what if none of it worked? What if the unthinkable happened? What if Toby died?

The thought made Jed feel faint and he dropped his head forward, taking deep breaths till the spots before his eyes cleared.

'Is he going to live?'

Aimee's sharp intake of breath reverberated around the room and she tried to smother it with a forced cough. As if the scenario the doctor had painted for them in plain, harsh language wasn't bad enough, he'd had to force the issue, to hear the reassurance he desperately craved.

He couldn't pinpoint the exact moment his mindset shifted but at some moment in time, as the doctor rambled on about treatment and prognosis, he'd suddenly realised that he wanted a chance with Toby. A chance at what he still hadn't figured out, but he knew that just meeting the little guy wouldn't be enough.

He may not know how to be a father.

He may not even want that kind of responsibility.

But right now he knew he wanted to take a chance and see what kind of man he was, what kind of a dad he could be.

And the realisation scared him to death.

The doctor pursed his lips in disapproval and sent him a glare over his specs. 'We can't give guarantees.'

'No, I guess not,' Jed said, the sudden realisation that even if he was compatible, that even if Toby underwent every form of lifesaving treatment known to man he could still die hit home with the force of a hurricane with the potential to leave as much devastation in its wake.

'Right. Let's get this underway, then.'

If the doctor had appeared cold and detached

before, he seemed positively frosty now. Must be his way of distancing himself in a world filled with bad news and worse.

'You OK?' Jed turned to Aimee as her hand fluttered nervously near her face, pushing a frizzy blonde strand out of her eyes, determined to show she wasn't intimidated despite the solemnity of the occasion.

He'd always admired that about her, her ability to take on anyone and anything. Bold, brash and undeniably feisty, his Aimee had been a woman going places. Unfortunately, she wasn't 'his Aimee' any longer and the only place they were both going for the next few months was straight to a living hell.

'Yeah, how about you?'

'I can do without the whole needle thing but I'm OK.'

Her lips twitched in a small, tight smile, drawing his attention to their shape, their fullness, reminding him how they had once contoured to his so perfectly. Before he felt

like an absolute bastard for remembering something like that when Toby's life was at stake.

'Still don't like needles, huh?'

'I'll survive,' he said, wanting to kick himself
for his poor choice of words as her mouth
drooped and she paled.

'I'm sorry—'

'If you'll follow me, we can get started.'
The doctor bustled back in the room, prevent-
ing him from trying to make up for that
horrible gaffe. Though what could he do—
take it back?

Hell. He hadn't even met Toby yet and he
was already bumbling along like a loser. What
hope did he have?

'Come on.' Aimee stood up, her movements
stiff and jerky, and before he knew what was
happening the doctor had ushered them out the
door and into the cold, sterile corridor that led
to a waiting room jam-packed with people.
People with pale faces, worried faces, people
hoping for a miracle just as they were.

'He's going to be OK. We have to believe that,' she said, her voice so soft he had to lean forward to catch her words, as if she was reciting an often practised mantra.

This was crazy.

A few hours ago he'd been a guy on top of the world, Australia's answer to Jamie Oliver, whipping up gourmet meals in his award-winning restaurant in Sydney while hosting his own TV series on a weekly basis. A guy who enjoyed life, who valued fine food, good wine and cherished his private down-time when he loved to sail. A guy who'd been looking forward to catching up with an old flame, curiosity quickening his heartbeat in anticipation as to why she'd wanted to see him.

Now all that had changed. That carefree guy had become a father, a father of a sick child, and nothing would ever be the same again.

'Your strength is amazing,' he said, wanting to cup Aimee's cheek, to savour the soft skin beneath his palm but unable to broach the huge emotional gap between them. That comforting hug back at the shop had only served to push them further apart; he'd been annoyed for being a softie when his anger was still raw and she'd looked downright uncomfortable. 'For what it's worth, I think you're spot on. Toby's going to be all right.'

He has to be, for all our sakes.

Her eyes misted but she didn't cry, the gold flecks shining through her unshed tears, her bravery setting a clamp around his heart and squeezing, hard.

'Yes, he's going to be all right,' she echoed, staring at him with fervent hope in her eyes, as he wished he had half her conviction.

Aimee slipped into Toby's room while Jed underwent testing, being careful not to wake her sleeping son. She tiptoed across the faded linoleum floor imprinted with bunnies, wrinkling her nose at the pungent disinfectant smell so characteristic of hospitals. She hated it. Give her the smell of warm chocolate, cinnamon and baking any day.

Reaching his bedside, she stood over her beautiful son, watching the gentle rise and fall of his chest, the dark blonde hair plastered to his scalp in messy whorls, his long eyelashes casting shadows against his pale cheeks. Swaddled in sheets, he looked so small, so helpless. So *sick*.

Toby had rarely been ill over the last five years, apart from a bout of chickenpox as a toddler and the occasional cold. He was a strong, resilient boy who loved to run along St Kilda beach, kicking his feet through the sand and frolicking in the waves during summer. He'd climb anything, jump off anything, his daredevil attitude leaving her with her heart in her mouth on several occasions.

But nothing like this.

Nothing like this totally useless feeling that

consumed her, that ate away at her till she wanted to scream. Her son could be dying and there wasn't one darn thing she could do about it.

Though contacting Jed had been proactive even if it was the last thing she'd wanted to do. She didn't want him in her life, in Toby's life. It could only lead to pain and disappointment and she'd already been there, done that.

Jed wasn't a family man. He didn't know the meaning of the word, while she'd raised Toby, built a flourishing business and created a comfortable home for them.

Uh-uh, there was no room for Jed in their lives yet fate had changed all that, had taken away her options.

And now he was here, bristling with anger, blaming her when he had no right. He'd given up his rights the minute he'd walked away from her without looking back.

Though at least he'd come when she'd asked and that had to count for something. Not only that, but she'd also seen him push aside his own feelings and concentrate on Toby, the son he'd just discovered. It took a big man to do that and, despite her own twisted bitterness towards him for ruining their future and breaking her heart in the process, she had to admire him for standing up when it counted.

Toby stirred, his head thrashing from side to side as if he was trapped in a nightmare. Her heart clenching with fear at the real, live nightmare they all faced over the next few months, she leaned forward, smoothed his brow and dropped a light kiss on his clammy forehead.

'I love you, Tobes,' she murmured, inhaling his little-boy smell the way she had used to when he was a baby, savouring their closeness, thanking God that he'd come into her life.

He snuffled and turned onto his side, snuggling into the blankets, a small smile playing around his mouth.

Yes, he was definitely a precious miracle she was thankful for every day. Now, if only Jed was compatible, the treatment worked and

Toby lived the long, happy life he deserved, that would be a true miracle indeed.

Stifling the sob that rose in her throat, she swiped at her tears and crept from the room.

And walked straight into the man who held Toby's life in his hands.

CHAPTER FOUR

'TOBY'S sleeping,' Aimee said, her gaze fixed on Jed's lapels.

She couldn't look him in the eye, not with the strange fluttering in her belly that began the minute he'd steadied her, his hands warm and firm against her bare upper arms. Darn it, she remembered that feeling all too well, the buzz of being held by him, the yearning to get closer.

But what was the deal now? Those feelings were long gone. She'd seen to that with the many nights she'd spent talking to the baby she carried, focusing on the new life growing inside her rather than the guy who'd helped create it. Being pregnant had been a godsend, channelling all her energy into a positive outcome rather than the assured pity party she would've thrown had she returned to Melbourne alone and broken-hearted.

'Is he OK?' Jed dropped his hands and looked at the door to Toby's room as if he wanted to barge in there and see for himself.

'Uh-huh. He's always been a good sleeper, thank goodness, so once he's out for the night he'll sleep right through.'

'Good.'

Their stilted conversation came to an abrupt end and she fiddled with the stitching on her bag, eager to escape Jed's intimidating presence but unsure how to extract herself gracefully.

He was here and he was here to help. She needed to remember that, no matter how uncomfortable he made her feel.

'I'm heading home,' she said, trying not to squirm under his intense stare. Why was he looking at her like that, as if sizing her up?

'Aren't you staying?'

She heard the censure in his voice, the silent

accusation that what sort of a mother was she to leave her sick child alone in hospital?

Hating her compulsion to justify herself to him, she said, 'I hate leaving Toby but sleeping on a fold-up bed next to his bed wouldn't help either of us. He's a bright boy; he knows he's unwell but not the severity of it. If I start staying over, he'll know something is dreadfully wrong and I don't want that. He needs to stay positive and I need to stay alert for the both of us.'

'I see.' By the thinness of his compressed lips, he didn't. 'What time will you be back in the morning? I'd like to meet our son.'

Our son.

Why did the sound of Jed's deep voice saying those two simple words have such a devastating effect on her?

Maybe because she'd always thought of Toby as hers.

Maybe because there hadn't been 'our' anything between them for so long.

Or maybe she was so darned scared of what letting Jed into their lives could do.

She needed calm right now, not havoc, and though Jed's presence here was important for medical reasons she could do without the emotional complication.

'I have to speak to Marsha, the manager at the shop, first thing in the morning but I should be here about ten.'

He didn't look happy. So what was new? He hadn't stopped giving her dirty looks since she'd told him about Toby, his anger a palpable entity that radiated off him in nasty waves and all directed at her.

'Look, I know this has to be tough on you but you're here now and waiting another twelve hours isn't going to make a difference.' She laid a tentative hand on his sleeve, once again annoyed at the little sizzle of heat that arced between them.

This couldn't be happening. It *shouldn't* be happening, not with Toby lying in there, fighting for life.

Dropping her hand quickly, she was unprepared for his light touch under her chin as he raised her face to look into his.

'Stop trying to tell me how I'm thinking or feeling. You don't know how tough this is on me. In fact, you don't know anything about me any more. So just drop it, OK?'

The pain in his eyes ripped into her and she blinked in an effort to shield herself from it. For a guy she'd assumed would make lousy father material, he sure was more emotionally connected than she'd given him credit for.

'I'm sorry.' Her whisper hung in the awkward silence between them, till the faint beeping of a patient's monitor disrupted the unnatural quiet in the corridor.

'Sorry for what? Sorry for lying to me all these years? Or sorry you're going to have to let me into Toby's life now?'

'That's unfair.' She averted her gaze quickly but his grip on her chin tightened, forcing her to look at him.

'Is it? Rather rich, seeing as I'm the one who should be crying unfair right about now.'

'Why are you doing this? Punishing me isn't going to help Toby. I thought we sorted the problems between you and me back at the shop.'

For a long, interminable second he stared into her eyes and the pain shifted, replaced by another emotion she couldn't define or didn't want to, as his gaze lowered to her lips for a moment before returning to lock on to hers.

Her heart tripped as his grip on her chin softened and he leaned towards her an infinitesimal inch, a subtle heat smouldering in his golden eyes.

No way. That banked heat had to be anger, disgust, anything other than need, surely?

And to make matters worse, her pulse raced at the thought.

'You don't know the meaning of punishment,' he said, his soft, minty breath fanning her face way too close before he dropped his hand and stepped away, running a hand through his hair and adding to the dishevelled air he'd had about him since the testing.

The test! She'd been so caught up in the awkwardness between them, she hadn't even asked how it had gone. As for his cryptic comment, she assumed he was referring to her not telling him about Toby and she chose to ignore it, too tired to fight any more.

'How did the testing go?'

He grimaced and showed her the back of his hand, where a faint purplish bruise was already taking shape. 'I hate needles for a reason. Damn medicos can never find a vein in my elbow crease so they always go for the back of my hand and it hurts like hell.'

'Poor baby,' she crooned, surprised by her urge to tease and even more surprised by her smile. That was twice in one evening he'd made her smile when she hadn't felt like it in days.

In a way, having Jed around could be a good thing and not just as a potential donor for Toby. If she was completely honest with herself, she liked having a male around who didn't depend on her totally, who could pick up the slack or who could just be there if she needed him. Not that she could count on Jed. She'd learned that the hard way.

'Guess a kiss to make it better is out of the question?' He held out his hand, staring at it in mock dismay as if the tiny bruise had developed into a giant haematoma.

Her lips twitched at the startling similarity between father and son, Toby pulling this same trick last month when he'd jammed his finger in the fridge door—while pilfering a vanilla slice she'd said no to!

'Maybe not.'

Jed's eyes were riveted to hers in wide-eyed shock as she kissed her fingertips and casually tapped them on the back of his hand. 'There, all better.'

Shaking his head, he thrust the all-better hand into his trouser pocket, glaring at her with irritation. 'You still confuse the hell out of me.'

Her smile faded as reality intruded.

The way she saw it, there had been no confusion in their happy relationship. Until she'd introduced the topic of forever and he'd started playing hide and seek, that was. Then there had been confusion and plenty of it, unfortunately all on her part.

'I have to go.'

Her sharp response shattered the last of any lingering camaraderie that she'd falsely created with her teasing. What had she been thinking anyway? Getting along with Jed for the sake of Toby was one thing, getting too familiar another.

It was his fault with that unexpected look he'd given her, the one which screamed 'I still think you're hot'. Or was it hers, a spot of wishful thinking tainting her reactions to the one man who had once rocked her world?

Either way, she needed to get out of here. Away from Jed, away from his all-seeing eyes, away from the temptation of staying by his side just because it felt so darn good to share her problems with someone else.

'I'll give you a lift,' he said, fishing his keys out of his pocket and standing back to let her lead the way.

'No!' she practically shouted before lowering her voice with effort as he raised an eyebrow. 'I'll take a taxi and you head back to your hotel. You must be exhausted after the day you've had. After all I've dumped on you. In fact—'

'Shh.' His finger against her lips stopped her babbling while kick-starting her pulse again. It hammered and tripped and pounded its way through veins suddenly way too small for all that blood, depriving her oxygen-starved brain of a much needed jolt.

'I'll drop you off. Besides, I'm staying at the Bayside Novotel just down the road from you. Come on.'

Why couldn't she move? Say something? Do something? She didn't want to be confined in his snazzy hire car. She didn't want to talk or smile or feel any of the other crazy things he'd made her feel over the last few hours.

She wanted to go home to bed, to think, to pray for her little boy and to forget every reason why this man made her feel so protected, so comforted, when he had no intention of sticking around for the long haul.

'Aimee? You're swaying on your feet. Let's go.'

The last of the fight drained out of her and she followed him, blowing a silent kiss in Toby's direction.

Her son would meet his father tomorrow and heaven help her if she didn't handle it a lot better than the last few hours with Jed.

Jed looked out of his hotel window, his absent-minded stare taking in the glittering lights of Melbourne in the distance, the sweep of the shoreline of Port Phillip Bay and the neon glow from bars and restaurants in a bustling St Kilda on his doorstep.

Usually he loved the bright lights, the razzle-dazzle of any city at night, and he'd been around the world to quite a few. Before his stint on Dunk Island and the events that had changed his life, he'd worked in Bali, Singapore and Hong Kong, cooking up a storm at various five-star hotels.

Then he'd met Aimee and nothing had ever been the same again.

Closing his eyes, he leaned his forehead against the cold glass, enjoying the cooling effect on his throbbing head. He had a blinder of a headache and, with the jumbled thoughts swirling through his mind, it looked as if it wouldn't abate in a hurry.

When he'd first walked into the patisserie earlier this evening and seen Aimee, his heart had slammed into his ribcage as the years rolled back. She looked the same: blonde curls in a tantalising mess around her heart-shaped face, hazel eyes crinkling at the corners while she was deep in thought, her full lips pursed ever so slightly.

Then she'd turned to face him and he knew he was wrong. She didn't look the same, she looked amazing, despite the smudge of icing sugar along her jaw and the dark rings of fatigue under her eyes. Not that they were any surprise, considering the bombshell she'd dropped on him.

He had a son. Toby.

And it was just as terrifying now as when she had first told him.

At least his anger had abated some, though he still felt like finding a kitchen somewhere and whipping up a gourmet meal for a hundred or so. Where his mates channelled their fury into kick-boxing and triathlons, he preferred whipping up a frenzy in the kitchen as an outlet for pent-up emotion, and man, was he on overload at the moment.

He'd barely absorbed the news he was Toby's father before Aimee lumped the rest of it on him, the worst part, about Toby's illness, and his anger had kicked in all over again.

What if his marrow wasn't compatible? What if he didn't know how to be a father at a time when Toby needed him the most? What if Toby hated him on sight?

Hell, he hadn't even got into that with Aimee. How much had she told Toby? Did the boy know he had a father and, if so, what was his excuse for staying away for the first five years of his life?

The pain in his head increased as he contemplated questions he had no answers to.

He'd had this trip all planned out: see Aimee, hear her out, try to rekindle some of their old magic and see what happened.

Though she wouldn't believe him, he'd changed. He'd done his duty, standing by his dad when he needed him the most. However, there wasn't much he could do now apart from paying regular visits to the prison and, while the rest of his life had taken off like a rocket for outer space, his personal life lacked spark.

Sure, he had women schmoozing up to him

all the time. TV did that for a bloke. But they were all fake, arm-candy types from the tops of their blonde foils to their nipped and tucked bottoms. He dated, he socialised but no one came close to filling the void Aimee had left when they'd split up and her urgent plea to see him couldn't have come at a better time.

So he'd thought.

Now he had a woman who still despised him for the secrets he'd had to keep years ago, a son whom he suddenly found himself wanting to know yet paralysed with fear of inadequacy, and a situation he had no control over.

That's bull and you know it. You've been in charge of your own destiny since you were fourteen years old and the old man did his first stint behind bars. You're in control. You always have been.

Jed blinked in surprise at the ferocity of his voice of reason but it did the trick. He straightened, rubbed a weary hand over his eyes and headed for his laptop.

He had things to do, a life to prioritise.

So what if he hadn't come to terms with his new role as a dad yet?

So what if he was so scared of failure he wanted to bolt back to Sydney as if none of this had ever happened?

The simple fact was, his son needed his help and he either stood up or wimped out, the second not an option.

Starting right now, Toby came first and everything else could be delegated or rescheduled. He may not be able to control the length of time he had with his son but by God he'd make every second count.

CHAPTER FIVE

AIMEE sat on an old wooden bench near the hospital entrance and sipped at her mocha latte, watching the parade of worried faces rushing past on a regular basis and wondering if she looked that bad. For Toby's sake, she hoped not. She'd done her best to shield him from pain while he was growing up, feeling she owed him something extra to make up for not having a father.

Sure, her own dad had been amazing with his grandson, but after he'd died she'd noticed the subtle changes in Toby's behaviour: he became more demanding, more cunning, more rough-house in his antics as if he could bully her into bending to his will.

She'd weathered the terrible twos, the tantrum threes and the frustrating fours, only to realise her son was gifted and needed more brain stimulation than the average child. Unfortunately, Toby's high IQ also ensured he observed a lot more than other kids his age and he'd been particularly demanding about his father recently. He'd accepted her excuse that his father was overseas for a long time but lately he'd been pushing. Little had she known he would get his wish to meet his dad sooner rather than later.

Speaking of which…she watched Jed stride towards her, his long legs eating up the pavement, a guy intent on going places. He hadn't seen her yet, his forehead puckered in concentration as he spoke into a mobile phone, using his free hand to emphasise his words to the person on the other end.

Warmth stole through her body and it had nothing to do with the morning sun blazing down its late-summer heat. Nor did it have anything to do with the casual beige chinos moulding his legs or the navy polo shirt fitting a muscular torso that didn't belong on a chef. Didn't he taste his own food? She had back then and had gained five kilos in six months!

No, it had everything to do with the fact he was here, as promised, his face lighting up the minute he spied her after slipping the phone into his pocket. Before a mask of impassivity slid into place, effectively shutting her out.

Great. She'd hoped he might've gained some perspective overnight, let some of his anger go, but it looked as though he'd been stewing. And it was her that was cooked, not some tasty piece of rib-eye he usually sautéed for the masses.

Though at least he'd returned. She'd had her doubts after he'd dropped her home last night. Many guys would've bolted like a fugitive into the night after the heavy stuff she'd dumped on him, and in a way his past behaviour in the running-away stakes hadn't exactly inspired her with confidence.

Yet here he was, looking annoyingly fresh— and sexy, though she banished that thought as quickly as it flashed through her head—ready to take the next step in their quest to save Toby.

'How you feeling?' He reached out a hand and helped her up, placing a quick kiss on her cheek before she could blink.

She knew it was a reflex reaction with him, something he did to all his friends. However, it didn't make it any less special, considering he'd been treating her like the enemy for withholding Toby from him all these years.

'I'm OK, I guess. I managed a few hours' sleep last night. How about you?'

'Not bad. Grabbed forty winks but I had a lot on my mind.'

Up close, she could see fatigue circles rimming his eyes, though they hadn't lost any of their lustre. It had something to do with the colour, that startling amber standing out like a gold beacon from his tanned face. The same striking colour she saw every day when she looked into her son's expressive eyes.

'Guess I had a lot to do with that, huh?'

He nodded, the simple action wrapping her in a faint waft of a spicy blend. His scent. The soap he'd always used. And the memories came flooding back in a barrage that almost had her reeling: snuggling into his arms at night, play-fighting over who got more of the blankets, him spooning her to sleep, sharing steamy showers... Each memory more evocative than the last.

But they were just that. Memories. Past snap-shots of a time long-forgotten and totally irrele-vant to their current situation, two people divided by an unbridgeable chasm yet joined in a valiant cause. One of life's little ironies which would've tickled her wry sense of humour if she hadn't been a major player in the drama about to unfold.

'What have you told Toby about me?'

Jed frowned and folded his arms, having dis-pensed with the niceties and stepping into the ring for round two, while her head still reeled from the round-one sparring last night.

'Nothing yet,' she admitted, bracing herself

for another stand-up, knock-down verbal assault but hoping to pre-empt it. 'That's what I wanted to talk to you about this morning. I know you're anxious to meet Toby but I need some time with him to explain a few things.'

His frown deepened and she knew he wouldn't give her an inch. 'Like what? How you kept us apart all these years? How I had no idea he existed? Or what a lousy father you think I'd make?'

'Grow up,' she snapped, the week of bad news, sleepless nights and tension-fraught reunions finally taking their toll. She'd tried to be adult about this situation but it looked as if Jed seemed hell-bent on dragging her over the coals. For the next twenty years, give or take ten.

'You want a piece of me? Fine. Give it your best shot. Say what's on your mind. Get rid of your anger. Do whatever it takes but for goodness' sake, let's move on. You don't have to like me. You don't even have to speak to me much but if you're willing to help Toby like you said last night, you'd better get a grip. And fast.'

She glared at him, daring him to argue, to continue what he'd started with his stupid, snide questions. Instead his frown vanished, to be replaced by a sheepish smirk that reminded her so much of Toby at his repentant best.

'You're right. I'm furious with you and that's probably not going to change for a while. You know I can't forgive you for what you've done and that's a definite. But the one thing I do know is that I want to help Toby despite my antagonism towards you. There, is that grown-up enough for you?'

'It'll do for now.' She pretended to huff when, in fact, her anger had deflated pretty quickly. He had enough of that emotion going on for the both of them and right now it was totally wasted. Toby was her priority, not his screwed-up father.

'You'd rather I didn't meet him, wouldn't you?' He stared at her, willing her to deny it but his mind made up anyway. She could see it in the set of his jaw, his rigid neck muscles and the steely glint in his eyes.

What could she say? That she'd hoped it wouldn't come to this, ever? That she'd hoped he'd donate his marrow if compatible and head back to his own well-ordered life, leaving them alone? That she'd be spared from a confrontation with her son that wouldn't be happening if she'd been honest from the start?

She'd pondered all these reasons and more when she'd made the decision to contact Jed and ask for his help, and unfortunately she couldn't give him the answers he hoped for.

'I don't want Toby hurt and if meeting you is going to do that, then no, I don't want you to meet him.'

He flinched ever so slightly at her in-your-face honesty, hurt flickering in the amber depths of his eyes. 'You expect me to waltz in there, say hi to the little guy, pretend I'm just your average, run-of-the-mill donor and waltz back out of his life?'

'I don't have any expectations where you're concerned,' she said, barely refraining from adding *not any more*. 'I guess I don't want Toby getting all excited about having a dad when you mightn't be around beyond this week or the next.'

Hurt hardened to cold, calculated fury, turning his eyes from amber to pure crystal gold.

'How about you give me some credit and I'll stop giving you a hard time?'

'Deal,' she said, wondering for the hundredth time since she'd seen him last night where the heck they'd gone wrong.

They'd been two people with the world at their feet, holding hands and ready to take the plunge into the unknown together. Before he'd jumped without her, leaving her to make do the best she could.

Her best was Toby and there was no way she'd let Jed hurt him, father or not.

'I'll smooth the way with him, then call you in, OK?'

'Fine. The doc wanted to see me anyway, so

I'll drop by his office and meet you outside Toby's room when you're ready.'

Her heart stalled at the gravity in his voice. 'Did the doctor mention anything about the test results?'

'No. I assume that's what he wants to talk about.'

'I'll come with you.' She almost grabbed his arm to drag him into the hospital but stopped at the last second, his serious expression brooking no argument.

'You go and see Toby, I'll take care of the doc,' he said, heading towards the hospital doors before she could respond.

'Jed, we're in this together.' She tried to keep the desperation out of her voice but he must've heard something to make him stop because he paused as the doors slid open and turned back.

'Nice of you to finally acknowledge the fact even if it is five years too late.'

With that parting shot, he headed through the electronic doors and didn't look back.

* * *

Aimee took a few steadying breaths outside Toby's room, pasted a smile on her face and breezed into her son's room, hoping she didn't look as frazzled as she felt. Dealing with Jed's animosity did that to her, as if she didn't have enough on her plate.

'Hey, Tobes. How's my little man today?'

'Mum!' Toby sat up in bed, his face a similar shade to the white sheet covering him. 'I'm OK but it's kind'a boring in here. And the nurse with the big nose keeps taking my temperature. And the one with the funny face keeps making me drink stuff when I don't want to. Yuck!'

Though Aimee smiled at Toby's words, her heart turned over at his fragility. Who was this boy? The astute judgement calls were definitely her son's but the pale face with huge golden eyes standing out like saucers seemed to belong to someone else altogether.

How had he deteriorated overnight? Was the

leukaemia so aggressive? If so, she prayed that Jed's visit to the doctor had a positive result. His marrow had to be compatible. It *had* to. She couldn't contemplate any other outcome.

'Sweetheart, the nurses are helping you to get better. You need to do what they say. And be polite to them.'

'I suppose.' Toby wrinkled his nose and fell back against the pillows, clearly exhausted from their brief conversation. 'Did you bring me anything?'

'Actually, I did.'

A flicker of interest brightened his dull eyes. 'What is it? Will I like it? Is it on my Christmas list?'

Her heart clenched with the hope in her son's eyes as she wondered if he'd rank having a dad up there alongside the latest train set, cricket bat or superhero jigsaw puzzle.

Wishing she could skirt around the issue—for the next fifteen years or so—she plunged straight in, all too aware that time was one luxury she didn't have. 'Tobes, remember when we discussed your dad?'

'Yeah?'

If he'd appeared interested in the possibility of toys, his eyes fairly bulged in anticipation of anything to do with his fabled father.

'Well, your dad's come back and he'd like to see you.'

'Oh, boy!' He struggled into a sitting position and grabbed hold of her hand. 'When? What's he like? Has he brought me a present? Is he staying long? Will he be living with us?'

The questions poured out of his mouth while his grip tightened, as if he expected her to vanish into thin air and take the answers to his questions with her. Little did he know, that was his father's trick, not hers.

As for Toby's innocent reference to how long Jed would be around, she hoped to God he wouldn't let his son down. Once Toby recovered—and he would, she wouldn't accept anything less—she'd make sure he didn't mess up with his son the way he had with her.

She squeezed Toby's hand and stroked the messy blonde spikes back from his face. 'He should be here pretty soon and he's really looking forward to meeting you. Remember when I said he was working overseas all this time? Well, he's back now and he wants to meet you.'

A tiny frown puckered Toby's brow and she yearned to kiss it away. However, that wouldn't go down too well, not when her son had decided smoochy kisses were 'uncool' over the last few months.

'Does he know I'm sick? He might not want to meet me while I'm in here.'

His face fell and it took every ounce of her will-power not to bundle him into her arms, cradle him close and never let go. 'Those nurses might try to take his temperature and make him drink yucky things and scare him away and everything.'

Unable to resist, she hugged Toby close and

planted a comforting kiss on the top of his head. 'He knows you're sick, sweetheart. Don't worry, everything's going to be OK.'

And as her son clung to her, his spindly arms wrapped tight around her neck, she hoped to God she was right.

Jed paced the corridor, wondering if he'd ever felt this nervous before. He'd faced some tough stuff as a kid, dealing with his dad's mood swings, raising his younger brother, keeping his dreams alive in the face of adversity and, later, finding the inner strength to walk away from Aimee, who had been the best thing to ever happen to him.

He'd survived the lot but nothing had made him feel as sick to the stomach as the prospect of what he'd find when he walked through that door and met his son for the first time.

Would the little guy like him? Or would he see straight through him with the knack that most kids had and label him a giant phoney?

Dads should feel a natural bond with their kids, should know what to say or do even when out of their depth. Yet right now, he felt none of it. No connection. He had no idea how to feel or what to say or how to act. And the awful thing was, the minute he walked through that door, he knew a smart kid like Toby would pick up on it.

Hell, stepping in front of the camera for the first time had been child's play compared to this.

What did he know about kids? *Really* know about them? He'd thought he'd known it all at one stage, raising Bud, but if the way his brother had turned out was any indication his fathering skills were on a par with that of his dad's honesty.

As he rounded the end of the corridor for his thirty-first lap, he heard the creak of a door and saw Aimee poke her head out. Trying not to bolt towards her, he willed one foot in front of the other, aiming for calm while his heart hammered in his chest.

When he neared, she caught sight of him and

slipped out of the room quickly, closing the door firmly behind her, and for a second it reminded him of the first time he'd visited his dad in jail and heard that final slam of the metal bars as they led him away. The sound sent a shiver down his spine and he stiffened, feeling as out of his depth now as he had then.

She beckoned him away from the door and, though he didn't want to admit it, relief shot through him at the momentary reprieve.

'What did the doctor say?' Her wide eyes pleaded with him, beseeched him for any scrap of positive news, and thankfully he could make this wish come true for her.

'I'm a match.'

'That's wonderful!'

She flung herself into his arms and he had no option but to hold her. But where did it say in the 'been there, done that' handbook that it had to feel so damn good, so right, to have her soft and pliant and moulding perfectly to him?

A tiny crack appeared in his angry armour

and he silently cursed. He didn't want to feel like this towards her. He had nothing but contempt for the way she'd treated him and he'd be a damn sight better off remembering what she thought of him rather than remembering the way they fit together like the yin and yang halves of a necklace he'd once given her.

Disengaging her arms, he stepped out of her embrace, annoyed he missed her touch and reacting accordingly. 'It's only a first step and there's a long way to go.'

'You're right.'

He hated seeing the fleeting happiness fade out of her eyes and he swore softly.

'How did it go in there?'

'Good. He's looking forward to meeting you.'

Feeling like a bungee jumper on the edge of a precipice with the rope tugging on his ankles, he said, 'What are we waiting for? Let's do it.'

CHAPTER SIX

THE moment Jed stepped into the claustrophobic hospital room and caught sight of the little boy propped up in bed, his world tilted and he knew straight away it would never right itself again.

Nothing could have prepared him for this.

No amount of parenting manuals, classes or DVDs, no amount of coaching from his expert friends who were the coolest of dads.

Nothing would have helped as he took one look at the pale face with the huge eyes the exact same shade as his own and tried not to reel back from the shock of seeing himself as a kid all those years ago, of feeling a tenuous connection that drew him to the bed like an invisible rope binding them.

'You're my dad?'

Toby's eyebrows shot up as he looked at Aimee for confirmation, doubt creasing his brow. 'But I know you! You're the cook Mum always watches on TV. You're famous!'

And before Jed could say anything, Toby's frown disappeared and he held his palm up for a high-five. 'How cool is that! My dad is famous.'

Jed tentatively slapped his palm against Toby's, racking his brain for some opening line, something half decent to say to this little boy who bore such a striking resemblance to himself.

'That's not a very good high-five. You need to practise them some more,' Toby said, studying his palm with interest. 'Maybe holding all those spoons and pots and pans and things have made your hand go soft.'

Jed laughed, a genuine warm sound at Toby's honesty, his nerves fading as he took the first step towards getting acquainted with his son.

'You could be right. Perhaps you could help me practise?'

'Yeah, that would be cool.' Toby's eyes

glowed with pleasure as something unfurled in the vicinity of Jed's heart. And that something was hope.

'Though I'm sick at the moment so maybe we could do it after I get out of here? Mum, when am I going home?'

Jed met Aimee's startled gaze over Toby's head, curious as to how she'd handle this. Right now, he needed all the parenting pointers he could get.

Aimee perched on the side of Toby's bed and smoothed his hair back from his forehead. 'The doctor will be coming by later; we can ask him then.'

'Oh.' Toby's face fell for a moment before brightening again. 'Maybe I can go home today? I'd like that. I can show D—' he stumbled for a moment, screwed up his brow and pointed at Jed '—him my car collection. And the cool kite I got for Christmas last year. And all my other stuff. Would that be OK?'

At the stricken look on Aimee's face, Jed

stepped in. 'We've got plenty of time for you to show me all your stuff, Toby. I'm not going anywhere.'

Once again, his gaze locked with Aimee's but this time his held a hint of challenge.

If she thought she could run him out of Toby's life after this, she had another think coming. He had no idea how he'd feel walking into this room but now he knew: he wanted to get to know the little guy sitting up in bed, an expression of false bravado on his face.

He mightn't know much about kids but he knew this: Toby was scared. It showed in his eyes, his pinched mouth and the way he clung to Aimee when she attempted to pull away.

'But you've already gone away before.' Toby's bottom lip thrust out and wobbled, making Jed feel like an ogre.

Though what could he say? *'Actually, this is all your mother's fault, son, as I didn't know you existed till yesterday'*?

Gritting his teeth against a sudden, renewed

surge of anger against Aimee, he said, 'I'm sticking around this time. I'm going to help you get better and then you can show me all that cool stuff you've got at home, OK?'

'OK.'

Toby slumped back against the pillows, his pale face almost blending in with the stark white cotton, a satisfied grin from ear to ear.

'You better get some rest, Tobes, and we'll come back with the doctor soon.'

Aimee bent and placed a kiss on Toby's head while Jed held his breath, wondering why the sight of his one-time soul-mate kissing her son—*their* son—should have such a profound effect. For one crazy second, he wanted to bundle them both in his arms in a huge group hug and never let go.

Damn, for a guy who'd taken a crack at the paternal thing and come up lacking, he sure felt way too close way too soon to this little boy.

'You sure you're coming back?' Toby shrugged out of Aimee's embrace and pinned him with a fierce look that said 'don't even think about lying to me'.

Wishing he could shrug off his feelings of total inadequacy, Jed went down on one knee next to the bed, bringing him to eye level with Toby. 'I sure am. Want to try another high-five to seal the deal?'

'You bet!'

This time, Jed put more oomph into his palm slapping, confident Toby could take it.

'Hey, that's not bad. With practice, you'll be as good as me in no time.' Toby's impressed grin made Jed feel ten feet tall, better than opening his first restaurant, better than serving a mouth-watering banquet to royalty and a hundred times better than he'd ever been made to feel by his own dysfunctional dad.

'See you later, champ.'

Toby's grin widened at being called champ, while Jed almost bit his tongue in frustration.

Damn it, where had that come from? Champ had been his nickname for Bud, and right now he didn't need any reminders of how raising his younger brother had turned out. He'd done his best but apparently, as Bud had reminded him on his first access visit to the juvenile detention centre, his best wasn't good enough.

Time to get out of here. Fast. Before he made a total hash of things when, all in all, meeting his son for the first time hadn't gone too badly.

Jed smiled at Toby, a flood of confusing feelings muddling his brain as he headed for the door behind Aimee. Should he feel more connected to his son? Should he feel more protective, more attuned, more *everything*?

Maybe his first instinct was right, that he'd be lousy at this father stuff? Perhaps he should donate the marrow, stick around to see if Toby pulled through and then do the easiest thing for them all and slip out of his life?

Then again, since when did he do easy?

'Hey!'

Jed stopped at the door and turned, surprised

by the volume of Toby's voice. For a young
guy, he sure had a bellow on him.

'You called me champ, which is really cool,
but I don't know what to call you.'

Jed's grip on the door handle tightened as he
floundered for an answer that would satisfy
them all. Was Jed too informal? Was Dad too
presumptuous and totally phoney, considering
his train of thought a few seconds ago?

Hell, he knew he was out of his league and
had no idea how to get up to scratch.

'What do you want to call him, Tobes?'
Aimee's calm, cool and collected voice put him
to shame. While he was mustering his thoughts,
desperately seeking the right answer, she sim-
plified the whole business in one, easy step.

He knew treating kids like adults was a way
to get them onside, a way to gain their respect,
and, by the straightening of Toby's stooped
shoulders, his mum knew exactly how to make
the little guy feel important.

'Would it be OK if I called you Dad?' Toby

said, his voice a mere whisper compared with its former volume, with a slight tremor to it as he stared at Jed with hope.

'Uh-huh,' Jed managed, before clearing his throat and saying, 'Sure, if you like,' as a lump the size of Ayers Rock lodged in his throat and wouldn't budge no matter how many times he swallowed.

'Cool.'

As Toby slumped back in his pillows and his eyelids fluttered shut, Jed followed Aimee out of the room, knowing that whatever happened, he wanted to live up to the important title his son had just bestowed on him.

Aimee tipped sugar into her cappuccino, wishing her problems would dissolve as easily as the tiny granules melting into the hot coffee.

She'd thought having Jed here might ease the burden a bit. She was wrong.

Having him meet Toby, seeing his reaction,

sensing the instant bond Toby had formed with his father sent a chill down her spine.

What had she done? Getting Jed's help to save Toby's life was one thing, risking him breaking their son's heart when he upped and left another.

'You stir that coffee any more and you'll have froth foaming over the side.'

Great. He wanted to lighten the mood, she wanted to question his intentions like some old-fashioned gun-toting father—or mother, in this case.

Laying her spoon down, she frowned at Jed and took a sip of her cappuccino before broaching the subject of why they were really here, sitting in a dingy hospital cafeteria trying to act as if their son wasn't ill or Jed didn't hold the power to save him in his hands.

Tired of the tension, she aimed straight for his jugular. 'You're a match. So are you willing to help Toby?'

He laid down his cup, the amusement she'd

glimpsed when he'd teased her about her fiddling fading fast. 'You don't mess around, do you?'

'We don't have time. Toby doesn't have time. Besides, I don't play games.' *Unlike you*, though she had the sense to keep that little gem to herself.

If he was angry, so was she, more furious than she'd thought possible for someone who had moved on. She'd tossed and turned all night, plagued by memories of how happy they'd once been, haunted by their catastrophic break-up.

Memories she could deal with.

Having him walk back into her life, looking so good, sounding the same, resurrecting a deep-seated yearning she'd fought so hard to get over, had sent her into a tail-spin. Darn right she was angry, at herself for being such a sentimental loser.

He ignored her jibe about game-playing, sat back and folded his arms, the cotton polo top outlining a set of biceps that belonged on a sportsman, not a chef, and she silently cursed herself for noticing.

'Honestly? If you'd asked me that last night, I have no idea how I would've answered. It was hard enough finding out about Toby, let alone thinking about anything else. Your deception had me so riled up I couldn't think straight and it took me a while to absorb everything. But now…'

He stopped abruptly, a strange expression flickering across the rugged planes of his face, something akin to fear mingled with tenderness.

'Now?' she prompted, nibbling on a fingernail while she waited impatiently for him to continue, knowing a lot of guys would hold a grudge for the secret she'd kept from him and hoping he wasn't one of them.

'Now that I know I'm compatible and I've had time to absorb everything, there's no question. I've told the doc to get things underway.'

'You told the doc?'

Relief flooded through her body that Jed had agreed to help, though something in his presumptuous tone made her response snappish rather than grateful.

'Get off your high horse, Aimee. I'm not trying to muscle in on your territory here, I'm doing the best I can after being slugged with a curve ball from left field. When are you going to cut me some slack?' He leaned forward, fixing her with a cold, hard stare, the kind of look she'd only seen from him once before, the night he had walked out on her without looking back.

And in some small, obtuse way, she was still making him pay for that.

Sure, she was worried he'd hurt Toby by leaving him with the same callous indifference he'd shown her, but deep down she knew most of her current animosity towards him sprang from her old pain rather than fear of what he'd do now.

'You're right.' She dropped her hands to her lap and clasped them tightly. No use showing him how completely he unnerved her. 'I'm taking a lot of my anxiety out on you when I should be grateful you're going to help.'

Tension drained out of his body as he sat back and reached for his coffee, though he hadn't unwound completely by the astute stare he sent her.

'If you think I'm going to hurt Toby, don't. He's a great kid and, though I may not be what you want in a father for him, I'm going to do what's right.'

'For how long?'

The words slipped out before she could think. So much for cutting him some slack.

'I don't know.' He shook his head, sorrow rather than anger darkening his eyes to burnished gold. 'Like you've said, I'm not father material so let's see how things go with Toby's treatment and we take it from there.'

'You know the treatment itself is going to take days but the danger period is a month?'

Now that she'd opened this particular can of worms, she couldn't leave it alone. Suddenly, she needed the reassurance that she'd been wrong about Jed, that she'd misjudged him. Maybe he'd be good for Toby and maybe, just maybe, he'd be there for her too in the gruelling months ahead when Toby's life hung in the balance?

He nodded, his gaze never leaving hers, as if he wanted to get his message across, and she hoped it was the one she wanted to hear.

'The doc explained it to me this morning. Toby has a few days' chemo to kill off the cancerous cells and bone marrow, then he gets the transplanted stuff from me. The two to four weeks after are critical and even if things go well, once he's home, it will take another six months for him to recover. All this time, he'll have frequent visits to the hospital for monitoring and further medicating if needed. It might take a year till the new bone marrow will function normally.'

'Wow, the doctor really gave you the full picture, didn't he?'

OK, so he'd impressed her. A lot. It had

taken her a few hours to process the info when she'd first heard it and here he was, reciting it back to her like a walking, talking version of *Gray's Anatomy*.

However, he hadn't really answered her question. Was he here for Toby's initial treatment or would he stick around for the long haul? Be there when the tough stuff really went down?

'As the doc said, it's best to be prepared and knowledge of what's in store can only help.'

'You sound like you've swallowed a medical dictionary,' she said, knowing it wasn't fair to push him for a time commitment but desperate to know where they stood. 'What about your business? It's not going to suffer with you being here for Toby's treatment?'

'The restaurant is fine for the next week and the TV show isn't shooting again till next autumn, so everything's under control.'

The next week.

For someone who'd wanted an answer so desperately, she wanted to cram his casual words straight back down his throat. A week. One lousy week was all he could spare to see how Toby went with the treatment.

She should've known. She *had* known but she'd gone ahead and bolstered her hopes anyway, thinking he'd changed, that things would be different for their son.

Fat chance. If anyone should know how futile hope could be, it was her.

She'd hoped he loved her as much as she loved him five years ago.

She'd hoped he'd marry her and they'd live happily ever after.

She'd hoped for the perfect love her parents had had.

Instead, look where hope had led her; to depend on a guy she should've known would let her down. Again.

'Toby's some kid,' he said, pride straightening his shoulders. 'You didn't tell me he looks just like me.'

'Yeah, poor kid.' She managed a tight smile,

trying to hide how totally let down she felt with his short stay.

'Hey, as I recall, you didn't think there was too much wrong with this face at one stage.'

He took hold of his chin and turned his face side to side, giving her ample opportunity to study his profile from all angles as she tried not to notice the cute little dimple in his right cheek, the dusting of dark stubble along his jaw that she'd loved scraped against her skin and the cheekbones that gave his face definition and screamed 'look at me'.

She'd looked all right, till his face had been imprinted on her brain through all the sleepless nights it took her to get over him.

'Ancient history.' She waved him away, hating the way her traitorous heart thudded at his cheeky grin, as if he knew exactly how he affected her and the history between them wasn't so ancient.

'Enough of the ancient stuff. These lines are testament to my wisdom.' He pointed to the laughter lines around his eyes, the ones she thought lent character to his once boyish face.

'Or testament to the murder of crows that have scratched around there.'

'Ouch!' He laughed and she joined in, shocked to hear the light-hearted sound come from her mouth. If she hadn't smiled in a while, it had been eons since she'd last laughed.

'That's better,' he said softly, reaching forward to capture her hand before staring at it in surprise and releasing it quickly. 'I remember you used to laugh all the time.'

She met his gaze unflinchingly, determined to ignore the lump of emotion his soft voice evoked and the fleeting warmth his reactive touch on her hand had left. 'Guess those days are long gone.'

'Yeah, guess you're right,' he said, regret mingled with something more potent radiating from his amber eyes, something closer to the intense passion they'd once shared so long ago.

Trying not to squirm beneath his stare, she

grasped at a quick change of subject. 'When's the procedure for the marrow extraction taking place?'

'Day after tomorrow.' He grimaced, looking so much like Toby when he had to eat broccoli that she chuckled again.

'You'll be under general anaesthetic so you won't feel a thing.'

'But they use a needle this long!' He held his hands two feet apart, rolling his eyes in mock exaggeration.

'Actually, you're wrong. It's this big.' Her arms spread a metre across and as he smiled she wondered what on earth they were doing, making light of the situation while Toby lay weak and helpless in a bed upstairs.

What was it about this guy that made her drop her guard, that made her feel comfortable when she'd been tied up in knots for the last week? Realistically, feeling guilty over making small talk or exchanging corny jokes to cope with the situation was silly and she knew it.

Having her collapse in an anxious heap wouldn't help Toby and, right now, he was her number-one priority. She should be thankful that Jed could help her lighten up, though with the years of resentment she harboured against him it was tough.

'You're going to enjoy my agony, aren't you?'

'Yep. I'm going to be first in line to slap you on the hip and withhold your pain medication afterwards.'

'Sadist.'

'No, just a woman scorned.' She'd aimed for flippant but, unfortunately, the words popped out sounding way too serious.

'I thought we were past all that.' He drained the last of his coffee, hiding behind his mug, an ineffectual shield if that was what he was using it for. Or perhaps he just wanted to finish up and get out of here yet here she was, second-guessing his motives the way she always had.

He was right. It was in the past. Time to move on.

'We are. Guess my sense of humour isn't up to scratch with everything going on.'

He nodded, his narrowed eyes the only indication that he hadn't bought her brush-off for a second.

'That's understandable. What are your plans for today?'

'I'm heading off to the shop for a few hours, then coming back here.'

She wanted to ask 'how about you?' but she'd given up keeping tabs on him a long time ago. She'd tried it once and look where that had got her: a boyfriend who'd started vanishing at regular intervals, covering up his whereabouts till she'd pushed her surveillance act so far that he'd run a mile. And never come back.

'If it's OK with you, I'd like to visit Toby again this afternoon?'

'With me?'

'Uh-huh.'

For a guy who appeared in control at all times, she sensed vulnerability in the way he fiddled with a serviette and the slight twitching of a tiny muscle in his jaw.

Ignoring the nervous flutter in her gut that allowing Jed too much time with Toby would only end in heartache for her little boy when he left, she said, 'OK,' hoping she was doing the right thing.

Though what choice did she have? Grab the guy's marrow and shove him out the door while he was still groggy from the op?

She'd started this by asking for his help and inviting him into their lives, and if the whole thing went belly-up she'd have to pick up the pieces.

'Good, that's settled.'

However, as he fell into stride beside her as they headed for the door, she knew nothing was settled.

Far from it.

CHAPTER SEVEN

'YUCK! My tummy feels like it does on the Mad Mouse at Luna Park.'

Toby held his belly and grimaced, his pale face taking on a greenish hue, and Jed wished for the hundredth time since this whole treatment business had started that this brave little kid didn't have to go through it. *His* brave little kid, a fact that still hadn't sunk in despite the daily visits and hours he'd spent trying to get to know him.

Hoping his own face didn't reflect Toby's as he watched his bone marrow travelling through the drip into Toby's arm, he said, 'Mad Mouse? What's that?'

Toby rolled his eyes. 'It's a roller coaster, Dad. Don't you know anything?'

'Oh, right. And Luna Park's in…America?'

This time, his silliness raised an exasperated smile out of his clever son. 'No! It's round the corner from my house. Maybe cooks don't know stuff like that.'

Jed smiled, knowing the twenty cooks who worked under him at his award-winning Sydney restaurant would love to hear their master chef being relegated back to cook status.

'You're probably right. My head's full of recipes and stuff like that. I don't know much about roller coasters.'

'Maybe when I'm all better, I could take you on Mad Mouse? And the scenic railway, which is even bigger! You don't need to be scared because I'll hold your hand, like how you've held my hand sometimes in here when that nasty nurse sticks stuff down this tube.'

Toby pointed to the catheter inserted in his chest just above his heart and Jed's gut roiled as it had for the last week every time he caught sight of it. Sure, he understood the need for the tube, as the medical staff constantly administered drugs, platelets and antibiotics to help prevent and fight off infection seeing as they'd crippled Toby's immune system with the chemotherapy in order for him to receive the bone marrow.

However, understanding the reasoning and seeing that tube piercing his son's body on a daily basis were two entirely different things and he felt an empathetic stab in the vicinity of his own heart every time he glanced at it.

'That'd be great.' Jed slipped his hand over Toby's and squeezed, an action that had freaked him out the first time he'd instinctively reached for his son's hand to comfort him yet didn't feel so alien any more. In fact, this comfort thing worked both ways and he derived satisfaction from the small hand clutching his, hanging on as if he'd never let go.

Satisfaction? A pretty emotionless word considering he'd run the gamut of emotions every time Toby had spoken to him, touched him or smiled at him over the last week. However, he didn't want to label what he was feeling. He couldn't. Acknowledging he had a son was one thing; thinking past the treatment phase of his illness another.

'Will this bone stuff of yours make me big and strong like you?'

Jed's heart clenched at the hope in Toby's voice and, though his faith hadn't been up to scratch since he'd been forced to make a choice between his family and Aimee, he sent a silent prayer heavenward for the umpteenth time that week.

'Do you think my bone stuff will give you muscles like this?' Jed struck a pose with his elbow bent, making his biceps bulge.

He nodded in encouragement as Toby reached out and squeezed his upper arm, the light brown eyes so like his own widening to saucer-like proportions.

'Wow! Your muscles are bigger than Superman's!'

'You think?'

Jed grinned, suddenly wishing Aimee was around. If Toby was good for his ego, she was the exact opposite, knocking him flatter than a pancake. They'd spent a lot of time together over the two weeks, though most of it had been here in Toby's room or in the depressing cafeteria, downing endless cups of average coffee, and her icy reserve towards him hadn't thawed in the slightest.

For a woman who'd once melted in his arms at the slightest provocation, she acted as if they were polite strangers and it annoyed the hell out of him. He didn't expect her to flirt or act coy or even like him but he wanted her respect. OK, he *needed* her respect, for it still galled him that she'd thought so little of him that he'd been deprived of knowing he had a son.

'You could wrestle the Incredible Hulk! And then you could fight Spiderman and Batman and the Phantom and everyone!' Toby's eyes gleamed and Jed leaned forward to ruffle his hair, knowing he'd have to put his resentment towards Aimee on the back burner at some stage, especially for this little guy's sake.

She'd been spot on at the start with her assessment of the situation. Toby was a bright kid and he would've picked up on any tension between them in an instant, which was why they'd gone to great lengths to always visit together and show a united front. Today was the first time he'd visited alone, a deliberate move on his part to push Aimee into realising something she should've recognised over a week ago: he might not be father material but he'd sure as hell like to try.

'You know, there's a superhero movie showing in the next few months. How about we go and watch the bad guys wrestle the good guys together?'

'That would be neat.'

However, by the slight frown between Toby's brows, Jed could tell that things weren't so neat.

'Don't you like the movies?'

Having to ask a question like that saddened

Jed beyond belief. He should know stuff like this and more, a whole lot more. But he didn't and it could take him a lifetime of playing catch-up and he still wouldn't know the small things, like Toby's favourite bath toy as a toddler or which leg he'd taken his first step with or how many nights he'd lain awake while teething.

Sure, he wouldn't have made the best dad in the world but Aimee had taken away his choice to try and that hurt. A lot. So much so he didn't think he'd ever be able to forgive her for it.

Toby opened his mouth and closed it again, leaving Jed feeling more helpless than ever. Should he push the little guy for an answer or try to distract him with a joke like earlier?

Toby's drooping bottom lip settled the dilemma for him in an instant.

'If you don't like movies, we can do something else. Your mum tells me you like kites. Or maybe we can go sailing. You like the beach, don't you? Or we could—'

'Are you going away again?'

Jed inwardly flinched at the directness of a question he had no idea how to answer. How could he reassure his son when he had no idea what he wanted to do himself?

Not that he hadn't considered the possibility of sticking around. He had, a million times over the last two weeks, but it always came back to the same thing: he'd tried being a dad once and it hadn't worked out. In fact, his relationship with his younger brother had gone pear-shaped because of it and he'd never recovered.

Could he risk ruining Toby's life if he mucked up again? Would he want to inflict that kind of long-lasting damage on his own flesh and blood?

The answer was a no-brainer yet every minute he spent in Toby's company he couldn't help but think that maybe he was wrong, maybe it would be better for Toby to have a dad around permanently than for a few access visits a year?

And if so, what would that mean for his relationship with Aimee? Would they even have one? It would take a monumental effort on both

sides: she'd need to let go of her disappointment in him letting her down and he'd need to
let go of his anger to forgive her.

No. He couldn't see this working much as
he'd examined it from every angle yet, with
Toby pinning him with that astute stare far
beyond his years, what could he say?

'Would you like me to stay around for a while?'

'Mum always tells me not to answer a
question with a question and you just did that.'

Jed bit back a grin. Nothing slipped past this
little guy.

Knowing Toby needed reassurance more
than anything right now, he squeezed his hand
and leaned forward to reinforce his words. 'I
know I haven't been around for you and I'm
sorry for that, but I'm going to make it up to
you. I promise.'

'You promise?'

'Promise.'

'OK, I guess that's cool and we can do all
that stuff you mentioned. Movies and kites

and sailing and stuff.' Toby paused, uncertainty flickering across his face, leaving Jed bracing himself for the next bombshell his son would drop. 'Cool stuff that normal dads do with their sons.'

'Sounds like a plan,' Jed said, knowing he'd never be a normal dad, no matter how much his son wanted it.

How could he be, when he didn't know how to live up to a label like that?

His grandfather had been a drunken old coot who beat up anyone within distance of his flying fists and his father had been teaching him and Bud tricks like pickpocketing and breaking into cars in their teens, slapping them on the back for mastering forging his signature rather than a straight-A report card. His dad had been in jail for more years of Jed's adult life than not and he'd taken Bud down with him, despite the years Jed had spent trying to instil ethics into his brother, showing him by example that the good guys always won.

Though in the fatherhood stakes, he'd lost and his confidence had never recovered.

'Dad?'

Jed started, as he wondered if he'd ever get used to being called that while intense, soul-stirring pride mingled with the shock of it all.

He was a dad, something he thought would never happen by his choice and, in a small way, he was grateful that the choice had been taken out of his hands, even by a woman who didn't have the right.

'Yes, Toby?'

'I am going to get better, aren't I?'

Damn, the punches kept coming and Jed had no option but to pick himself up off the canvas and take them like the man—like the father—he was supposed to be.

'You sure are and we're going to do all that stuff we talked about, OK?'

'OK.' Toby snuggled into his arms and Jed tensed, forcing himself to relax and hug his son back.

If verbal encouragement from his father had been non-existent, physical reassurance had been a pipedream. His dad had never hugged him, till the day his last sentence had come through and old Larry had finally broken down, blubbering like a baby that he was sorry for everything he'd put his family through, hanging on to Jed as if he were a lifeline with the outside world.

And he still would be that lifeline till his father's release in six months' time.

'I'm glad you came back,' Toby said softly, his words muffled against Jed's chest, and for the first time since he'd discovered he had a son Jed felt the first flickering of paternal love.

Aimee watched Jed cuddle Toby, angrily swiping at the tears trickling down her face while wanting to run in there and tear the two men in her life apart.

Since when did Jed spend one-on-one time with Toby, let alone cuddle him like a real father should? Sure, he'd visited Toby every day and been with her every step of the way in the gruelling treatment regimen to date but that was just it. He'd been *with her* every time he'd been near Toby and she guessed he was floundering out of his depth, totally unsure how to relate to his son.

Yet looking at the two of them right now, snuggled up to each other, she might have been wrong. Jed had spent the last ten minutes chatting with Toby, holding his hand and, by the smile on Toby's face, making him laugh. He appeared totally at ease with their son but then, appearances could be deceiving. Look how he'd deceived her.

'Toby's doing remarkably well.'

Aimee turned towards the voice she'd come to dread over the last month, managing a tight smile for Toby's oncologist, Jason Christie.

'He's a tough little boy.'

'Having his father as a perfect donor match was a stroke of luck.'

'Yes.'

'They seem to be getting along well.'

'Uh-huh.'

'You don't seem so thrilled about that.'

Aimee tore her gaze away from the father-and-son bonding session taking place in front of her eyes and looked at Jason—they'd moved way past the Dr Christie stage once Toby's treatment had begun in earnest—surprised he had the time to make more than a moment's small talk and even more surprised by his accurate assumption.

'You know Jed hasn't been around for Toby. I guess I'm just worried he'll take off again when this is all over and break Toby's heart.'

Jason cleared his throat and fiddled with the stethoscope around his neck. 'Please don't think I'm overstepping my mark here but I got the impression you chose not to let Toby's father into his life until now. What makes you think he'll leave again?'

Because that's what he does.

At least, that was what he'd done in the past and he hadn't said anything over the last two

weeks to change her mind, even if his allocated
week of sticking around had been and gone.
She hadn't broached the subject again and he
hadn't ventured any further information.
They'd co-existed in a weird bubble of anxiety,
all their attention focused on Toby and getting
him through the chemotherapy and transplant.
They'd bonded and perhaps this was what
frightened her the most.

Tiny cracks had splintered the icy wall she'd
built around her heart towards Jed and, as hard
as she tried to refreeze, it just wasn't happening. His dedication to helping Toby, his self-
lessness in dropping everything to be here, had
impressed her more than she cared to admit.

Though there was more to it and she knew it.

Toby wasn't the only one Jed was supporting
through this hard time; he'd been there for her
too, listening to her fears, distracting her with
his corny humour when she needed it, being
strong when her resolve weakened and her
hopes flagged.

All in all, Jed had wiggled his way back into a tiny part of her heart and it terrified her.

Sighing, Aimee opted for honesty, tired of bottling up her fears and battling them during the wee small hours of every morning when she couldn't sleep for worrying about her son and stressing over his father.

'I guess letting Jed into our lives has been a big step and I'm scared the whole thing will go belly-up.'

Jason smiled and laid a comforting hand on her shoulder. 'You can take or leave my opinion but I've been around people for a long time. I've delivered diagnoses, treated terminal patients and helped their grieving families through some of the toughest times of their lives. I've seen how people react, how they cope and, for what it's worth, Jed is handling all this very well. He appears to be one of the good guys and I seriously doubt he'd do anything to hurt that little boy of yours. So hang on in there. Stop beating yourself up over a decision that has turned into a life-saving one for Toby and concentrate on looking after yourself and that little battler in there.'

'Taking a psychology course in all your spare time, huh?'

He chuckled, took a quick glance at the pager clipped to his pocket as it shrilled three times and gave her shoulder a final pat. 'You'll be fine. I need to check on another patient but I'll be back to see Toby as soon as I can.'

'Thanks.'

She nodded, somewhat relieved at voicing her fears out loud and having someone as knowledgeable as Jason not laugh at her outright. Though he probably wouldn't do that even if he did find her pathetic. Must be something in their Hippopotamus oath—at least, that was what she'd named it when Toby had asked her how come doctors knew so much stuff. Of course, her smart son had wrinkled his nose at her blatant bluff and said he'd ask Dr Christie himself before drifting into another of his fitful dozes, leaving her clasping his hand and hoping for a miracle.

Staring into the room as Jed disengaged from Toby, pulled the bedclothes up and ruffled his hair before heading for the door, she thought that maybe she'd just witnessed one.

CHAPTER EIGHT

'COME in and take a seat. We need to talk.'

Dr Christie motioned them into his office, searching through a mountain of files on his desk while maintaining a monologue into a Dictaphone.

Aimee managed a wry smile as she walked ahead of Jed while he held open the door. Usually, it was a woman's prerogative to use the old 'we need to talk' line and it often signalled the end of a relationship. In this case, after daily chats with Jason about Toby's improving status over the last two months, she knew their relationship wasn't ending but she sure hoped for the frequency of their meetings to lessen, starting with taking her son home.

'Sounds ominous,' Jed muttered, holding out

a chair and waiting till she sat before taking a seat himself.

For a self-sufficient woman, she loved Jed's chivalry. Always had, finding the little touches like holding open a door or letting her pass first strangely antiquated in the twenty-first century but loving it all the same. It made her feel feminine, special, two things she hadn't felt in a long time.

Since he last spoiled you. Before leaving, that is.

Annoyed at her voice of reason putting a dampener on what promised to be a good day, she smiled at him. 'Don't worry. You know what's been going on. This has to be a formality before we get the discharge process happening.'

'You're probably right,' Jed said, running a hand over his day-old stubble, an action she'd seen countless times over the last few weeks as they'd shared a coffee, had a quick snack or played draughts next to Toby's bed.

Unfortunately, the last few times he'd done it

she'd become acutely aware of the rasp of
stubble against his palm and exactly how that
would feel against her own skin. How it had
used to feel against her skin…

Crazy, stupid thoughts that she blamed on the
intensity of the situation, forcing them to spend
so much time together, encouraging them to
bond and stand united for Toby's sake.

'I'm always right. Didn't you know?'

He snapped his fingers, his answering smile
warming her heart way more than it should. 'I
forgot. But not to worry, I'm sure you'll remind
me every chance you get.'

'You bet.'

The doctor's loud throat-clearing interrupted
their teasing and Aimee turned to face Jason,
wondering when she'd last felt this relaxed.
Toby wasn't out of the woods yet but his steady
improvement, culminating in their meeting
today, had lightened her heart till it could float
out of her chest.

'You both know how well Toby's doing but I

thought I'd run through some technical stuff, just so we all know what's ahead of us, OK?'

'Go ahead,' Jed said, his thumbs-up sign of encouragement under the desk making her want to giggle like a schoolgirl.

'Right. You know we did extensive tests on Toby's heart, kidneys, lungs and other vital organs before the transplant to get a baseline for comparison post-transplant? Well, I'm pleased to say that, two months post-BMT, Toby's organs are functioning well and haven't been impaired.'

'Thank God,' Aimee said, reaching for Jed's hand before she knew what she was doing and pulling back at the last second.

What she hadn't banked on was the same, instinctive reaction from him and as his long, strong fingers slid between hers, infusing her with his solid warmth, her heart thawed a fraction more.

'From the daily blood samples, it looks like the bone marrow has engrafted and is producing a sufficient number of normal red and white

blood cells, so we can take Toby off the anti-
biotic, blood and platelet transfusions and he
can go home.'

Jed's, 'Great news!' beat her, 'That's
fabulous!' by a split-second.

Jason smiled, obviously sharing their enthusiasm before he held up a hand. 'Though we've
got a long way to go yet. His recovery will
continue at home for the next few months at
least. He'll still be weak and probably won't be
able to do much more than sit up and walk
short distances. He'll need to come back here
as an outpatient several times a week for monitoring and medicating as needed, and overall
it can take some kids up to a year till they're
functioning normally again.'

Jed squeezed her hand and she returned the
gesture. However, as serious as the doctor's
words were, she couldn't help the thrill of ex-
hilaration racing through her body.

Toby was alive.

He was going to be OK and, though the

recovery process would be long and arduous, her precious little boy would be all right and she could kiss the man responsible.

As foolish as that would be!

When she raised her eyes to Jed's, the amber glow of happiness reflecting in his stare implied he knew exactly how she felt at that moment and her heart thudded in response.

Tearing her gaze away from Jed's hypnotic stare, she said, 'So that's it? We can take Toby home?'

'That's it,' Jason said, grinning at them like a benign Father Christmas who'd just made all their wishes come true.

'Thanks, doc. For everything.' Jed pumped Jason's hand with his free hand, not releasing his hold on her for a second.

'Thanks, Jason,' she echoed, knowing the words were totally inadequate for what they owed this man but finding the simple act of stringing words together in her delirious state almost impossible.

'My pleasure. Once the discharge summary is written up, you're free to go. I'll drop by and see Toby in a few minutes.'

Aimee stared at her hand joined with Jed's, wondering how it could feel so comfortable, so right, when they hadn't held hands in such a long time.

And petrified at how she'd feel when he released her. For good.

'Oh, one more thing.'

Aimee used Jason's interruption to slip her hand out of Jed's grasp, needing physical distance to gather her thoughts. Touching the guy for reassurance was one thing, hanging on when the doctor left the room another.

Besides, she'd been so caught up in the euphoria of Toby's discharge that she hadn't thought past one vital fact: now that their son was on the mend, wouldn't that signal the end of Jed's involvement in Toby's treatment? Wouldn't he leave, just as he'd said at the start?

Sobered by how devastated she felt at the

thought of Jed's impending departure, she folded her arms and turned away from him, a purely defensive gesture against the man who'd breached her defences without trying.

'Yes?'

'Toby needs a stable home environment to aid his recovery, so minimal stress and upheaval. Though, by the time you two have put in here, I'm preaching to the converted and I'm sure you'll do what's best for him. Good luck.'

And as Aimee followed the doctor out of the room, with Jed's astute gaze boring holes into her back, she knew she'd need every ounce of that luck.

'You OK?' Jed stopped her with a gentle tug on her hand, reinforcing how much she liked having her hand held by him, a fact she needed to remedy—and quick—if she had to string two coherent words together and respond.

His eyes blazed with emotion, drawing her in, telling her exactly how affected he'd been by the doctor's good news, and another piece of her heart thawed.

'The best I've been in a long time,' she said, torn between wanting to hug him for the role he'd played in saving Toby's life and interrogating him about his intentions from here.

'I know how you feel.'

She seriously doubted that, unless his stomach churned with elation, fear and dread. Elation for Toby, fear that Jed would now walk out of their lives and dread at how she'd handle the situation with a little boy who had opened his heart to his father.

'You heard what the doc said about a stable home environment?' Doubt flashed across his face and she braced herself for his next words, expecting to hear 'I'm out of here'.

'Uh-huh?'

'I think I should move in.' The words fell out of his mouth in a rush and she gaped at him, trying to equate what she'd just heard with what she'd expected to hear, her mind spinning when the two didn't compute. 'For Toby's sake. You know, to provide him with a stable home environment, a proper family.'

She stared at him in horror, seeing the earnest, almost desperate look on his face, knowing he'd lost his mind. Either that or he thought she'd lost hers. For a guy who couldn't give her straight answers about his plans—or their past for that matter—he thought she'd let him near her home, to let Toby get further attached, only to have Jed walk out when Toby's recovery was complete?

No way.

As for her own peace of mind, the idea of sharing their small apartment over the shop with Jed's larger-than-life presence even for a short space of time didn't bear thinking about.

Her feelings towards him might have softened but that didn't make her a masochist. Seeing him on a daily basis, sharing Toby's life with him, bonding the way they had was bad enough without having him in her face twenty-four-seven.

Wrenching her hand out of his, she folded her arms around her middle, deriving small comfort from the defensive gesture.

'You're out of your mind,' she said, calming her voice with effort when a passing nurse cast them a curious glance. 'Toby has a stable home environment, one *I've* created, no thanks to you. Yes, you're part of his life now and I see how much that means to him but that's where it ends for now. What do you think it would do to him to have you around every day while he recovers, only to have you do a runner when he's better?'

His eyes darkened to burnt caramel, wary, watchful. 'It doesn't have to be like that.'

'Really? So you planning to stick around forever, huh? And where does that leave us? Casual roomies?' Her temper spiked at the gall of his suggestion, at his implication that he'd stay for the long haul. If there was one thing she knew about Jed, he didn't do forever.

He reached out to her as if to placate her and

she shrugged off his touch. 'Look, I just thought—'

'No, you didn't think. If you had, you wouldn't have made such a stupid suggestion and I don't want to hear you bring it up again. You want to help Toby, to support him? Be there for him, listen to him, do the stuff you've already been doing.'

'What if it's not enough?' His quiet words pierced her protective armour, stabbing her where it hurt most, in the abundant, never-ending well of love she had for her son.

What if Jed was right? What if the home environment she'd created for him wasn't enough to sustain him in the tough months ahead?

Pushing her doubts firmly aside, she said, 'It will be. We'll make sure of it.'

He didn't look convinced but at least he had the grace to back down. 'Fine. It was just a thought. Friends?'

She stared at his outstretched hand, realising he wanted them to revert to their previous relationship before his ludicrous suggestion, casual, supportive *friends,* knowing she'd be hard-pressed to act as though nothing had happened but willing to make the effort for Toby's sake.

'Friends,' she said, slipping her hand briefly into his, hating how good it felt, wondering if she'd ever grow immune to this man and the potential havoc he could wreak on her life.

'Wow! My room's different.' Toby turned a slow three-sixty, making Jed and Aimee do the same as he clutched their hands. 'There's a new Batman poster and a Superman game and a huge kite!'

He suddenly stopped, a tiny frown creasing his brow as he nibbled his bottom lip. 'How come Santa brought all this stuff early? Does that mean I get nothing on Christmas Day?'

Aimee sent Jed a reassuring wink over Toby's head as indecision warred with confusion on his face. He'd bought all this stuff to brighten up

Toby's room for his homecoming but she could see he had no idea how to field Toby's question.

'Toby, Santa didn't bring all this stuff, Jed did. He wanted to surprise you.'

'Really? That's awesome. Thanks, Dad.' Toby's look of adoration as Jed crouched down and hugged him brought a lump to Aimee's throat.

The natural way father and son fit together, the joy in Toby's face and the enthusiastic rather than tentative hug from Jed all served to drive another dagger of fear into her heart. How soon would this end? And would she be left picking up the pieces again, though this time coping with Toby's broken heart too?

Thankfully, they'd moved past that awkward scene outside the doctor's office when she'd shot his idea to move in with them down in scorching, red-hot flames. In fact, they were both acting as if it had never happened, which was just fine with her. However, that didn't mean he couldn't give her answers about his plans for the future anyway.

Preparing for Toby's discharge had taken up most of her time since meeting with the doctor yesterday and she hadn't had a chance to confront Jed after his ridiculous proposition. In reality, she'd been meaning to approach him for the last week or so but had never found the right time.

Liar!

So she was a chicken too.

There had been a few opportunities over snatched snacks or coffees to ask him whether he intended on sticking around for longer but she'd happily avoided the topic, enjoying the rather unusual truce they'd achieved without trying.

They had slipped into a comfortable friendship, supporting each other, listening to each other, brought together by the common bond of Toby.

Comfortable schmomfortable!

OK, so she was telling fibs here too.

She wasn't comfortable in Jed's presence. In fact, the opposite. The more time she spent with him, the harder it was to maintain her distance, to keep up the icy barriers around her heart and, unfortunately, she could feel a heatwave coming along that could cause a major meltdown once and for all.

If she was completely honest, hadn't that been one of the motivating factors behind her absolute horror at his suggestion to move in? She could handle a visiting Jed. A live-in Jed would be disastrous!

'Into bed now, sweetheart. You know what Dr Christie said.' She didn't mean to sound so brisk but the mere thought of her resistance to Jed waning sent her into a tailspin.

And, by his raised eyebrow as he casually straightened, he knew it too.

Toby rolled his eyes but climbed into bed. 'I remember, Mum. He said I'm still a bit sick and I have to be careful of catching germs and I have to listen to what you say and not overdo things. Did I miss anything?'

Jed grinned, obviously impressed by the matter-of-fact way Toby ticked the points off on his small fingers.

That was another thing she'd enjoyed sharing with Jed: his pride in their son. In a way, she took Toby's cleverness for granted, his advanced ways a huge help for a single mum. He learned so quickly that she gave her little man more responsibility than usual for a child his age and he never complained, helping her in so many ways, bringing joy to her life when she'd had none.

Now the killjoy was back and could easily wreak further havoc if she let him.

'What about eating all your vegetables? I remember the doc saying that,' Jed said, bending down to tuck the bedclothes around Toby.

'Maybe. He also said I should have loads of ice cream.'

Once again, Jed sent a confused glance her way but she merely smiled, leaving him to get out of this one on his own.

'When did he say that?'

'When you and Mum weren't in the room.'

Aimee didn't buy Toby's smug grin for a moment and thankfully Jed had cottoned on to this parenting thing a lot better than she'd given him credit for.

'Really?'

'Yep.' Toby folded his arms and nodded so hard, his head almost hit the bookshelf behind the propped pillows.

'Oh.' Jed paused and tapped his chin, as if deep in thought. 'Remember that superhero code we talked about? The one where you and me always tell each other the truth?'

'Uh-huh.' Toby's smug smile slipped several notches as Aimee silently cheered Jed for the way he was handling this.

'Maybe the doctor said you could have stuff like ice cream sometimes and you got the message muddled up?'

'I think you're right, Dad,' Toby said, so grateful to be let off the hook that easily he snuggled into bed and pulled the bedclothes higher. 'I think I'll just have ice cream sometimes. After I eat my veggies,' he added, trying to sweeten them further.

'Good boy.' Jed ruffled Toby's hair, dropped a kiss on his head and turned to her, his smile reminiscent of his son's self-satisfied one a few moments earlier.

'Why don't you head downstairs and make a start on that coffee we talked about before and I'll be down shortly?'

'Sure.' Jed sent a smart salute at Toby, who giggled, and brushed past her on his way out the door, giving her arm a reassuring squeeze.

At least, she was sure that was how he meant it. Little did he know the bizarre connotation her dormant hormones put on it as they leaped to life and started partying.

'Dad's pretty cool, isn't he?'

'I'm glad you think so, Tobes.'

She sat on the edge of the bed and ran a hand over his forehead, a gentle, affectionate sweep that doubled as a quick check of his temperature. As far as Toby had come following the transplant, she knew the slightest cough or rise in his temperature would send her back into full-fledged panic mode over the next few months.

She knew Jed would tell her to chill out, which was easy for the king of cool to say.

He hadn't spent sleepless nights with a teething toddler who screamed as molars pierced tender gums, or cradled a sick child who couldn't breathe in a steam-filled bathroom to ease a bout of croup.

He hadn't fought back tears at a child's forlorn wave and look back on the first day of nursery or soothed when a bully had kicked over his first sandcastle.

And whose fault is that?

Ignoring her voice of reason, whose calm logic annoyed her at the best of times, she leaned forward to kiss Toby's cheek.

'You have a good rest and I'll bring you up something yummy for dinner.'

'A chocolate éclair?'

'No.'

'Apple strudel?'

'Toby…'

'A vanilla slice? That's your favourite, Mum, and we could share it.'

Chuckling, she smoothed the bedclothes and stood. 'You're too smart, mister. I was thinking more along the lines of minestrone soup and some stewed apple.'

Toby opened his mouth to protest, saw her stern look and murmured, 'Yes, Mum.'

'OK, then.'

She headed for the door, drinking in the sight of Toby's faded Spiderman wallpaper border, his higgledy-piggledy pile of stuffed animals on a bookshelf, his first train set vying for space with a Tonka truck in a corner. While he'd been in hospital, she hadn't come into this room, too afraid that the memories of her healthy, lively son would overwhelm her and she wouldn't be able to cope with the reality of his illness.

Now she could happily cartwheel around the room, taking each of his toys for a spin.

'Mum?'

'Yes, love?'

She paused at the door, saving the best sight for last, that of her precious son with colour in his cheeks and a sparkle in his eyes, tucked into his bed, exactly where he should be.

'Is Dad going to stay with us?'

The million-dollar question.

Unfortunately, she didn't have a clue to the answer.

'We're going to discuss important stuff like that but for now you concentrate on getting better, OK?'

Crossing her fingers behind her back that her astute son would buy her evasive yet honest answer, she held her breath.

'OK,' Toby said after a moment's pause, his eyelids drifting shut as she inched out the door, relieved that she'd bought some time.

But how much? And for how long?

Heading down the stairs, she knew it was time to ask Jed the tough questions even if she didn't want to hear his answers.

CHAPTER NINE

'I'M GLAD you agreed to have dinner with me.' Jed escorted Aimee into a corner booth, sliding onto the worn vinyl bench seat opposite. 'But Greasy Joe's? What sort of food does this place serve?'

Aimee waved at several waiters she knew by name, picked up a menu and handed it to Jed. 'The best, Mr Snobby Chef. Here, see for yourself. As for having dinner with you, it's the only way I could keep you and Toby from ganging up on me any more.'

At the mention of Toby's name, Jed's eyes took on a gaga look she would never have thought possible. 'He's some kid.'

'So you keep saying.'

Their gazes locked across the table, his a clear caramel, hers a confused hazel.

She didn't want to do this—spend an evening sitting across from him, smiling, chatting and trying to act as if he didn't affect her, when in reality her stomach churned with pent-up tension.

She'd fussed over her hair, her make-up and her outfit, something she hadn't done in ages. Sure, she'd dated a bit, but somehow, going out to dinner with Jed made the act of simple decision-making far too complicated.

After way too much dithering, she'd opted for the natural look with her wayward curls, using a ton of anti-frizz serum to tame them, and a quick slick of cherry gloss over her lips and a mascara wand over her lashes. She wasn't trying to impress him.

Oh, yeah? Then what's with the killer outfit?

OK, so maybe she'd been a tad obsessive with the clothes thing, but hey, a girl had to have one weakness, right?

Unfortunately, he was looking straight at her, appreciation for her fitted pale pink dress clear from the subtle yet sexy glint in his eyes.

'You know I only agreed to this dinner because you played dirty and I had no choice.'

If she'd thought her blunt talking would distract him long enough to stop him staring at her as if she were an entrée, she was wrong.

'Just because Toby happened to think it's a good idea I take you out for a break too doesn't mean I didn't play fair. You had a choice. You could've said no.'

And give up a chance to ask the hard questions she'd avoided the last few days since Toby had come home? No way.

She'd been fired up on several occasions, wanting to pin him down for Toby's sake. He had every right to know if his father intended on being part of his life long-term and she'd do anything to make Toby's recovery as smooth as possible.

Anything?

A vivid vision of getting up close and personal with Jed again flashed across her mind and she blinked, rapidly dispelling it. Maybe she needed to amend her good intentions to 'anything within reason'.

'I could've said no but there wouldn't have been any fun in that. I intend to grill you and here is as good a place as any.'

The corners of his mouth twitched, drawing her unwitting attention to his lips and the host of memories they could elicit on their own, given half a chance.

'Ah, so that's why you chose this place— Greasy Joe's Bar and Grill—though I had no idea I was on the menu.'

'I chose this place because it's within quick walking distance to home, just in case Toby needs me.'

His smile waned and he reached across the table to take hold of her hand before thinking better of it, thank goodness. Having him touch her to comfort had been OK. Now, in the cosy confines of a corner booth with the muted light, salsa music and the way he made her feel as if she was the only woman in the world when he looked at her with those amazing eyes, being touched would be way too dangerous.

It could lead to all sorts of crazy ideas, the primary one being how much she'd liked having Jed stick around. And not just for Toby's sake.

'You've done a great job with Toby and I'm not just talking about the last few months since he's been sick, so how about you cut yourself some slack and enjoy tonight? Let's not talk about hospitals or treatment and consider this a celebration of Toby's recovery to date. When was the last time you ate out anyway?'

'I get out.' She reached for a menu, knocking over the mustard, ketchup and salt shaker in the process.

'I can see that.'

His teasing grin had the potential to annoy her. Instead, she decided to take his advice and relax. Toby was in good hands. Marsha had been his nanny since her parents died and he really loved her. Not only was she a whizz with Toby, but Marsha also managed to run the pa-

tisserie when she needed time off, which had
been plenty over the last few months. Aimee
had no idea what she'd do without her and
hopefully she'd never find out.

Rearranging the tableware, she sent Jed a
flirtatious glance from under her lashes, a
look designed to show him that she did get
out—occasionally.

'What about you? I bet you do your fair share
of wining and dining, what with your reputation.'

'My reputation?'

'Don't play coy with me, Mr Australia's
Sexiest Chef.'

A faint pink stained his tanned cheeks, giving
him an adorable air of vulnerability as her pulse
picked up tempo.

Darn it, she knew this relaxing thing wouldn't
be a good idea. If he looked appealing before,
he appeared downright delicious with her new
and improved outlook.

'That was some bogus label the media
drummed up to get more ratings for the show.

Haven't you ever heard the old saying "don't believe everything you read"?'

'I didn't read it. Marsha said her friends talk about you all the time. They plan dinner parties using your menus but somehow nothing turns out the same as your stuff. They say it's your sex appeal that makes the food more attractive.'

'Hey! That's not fair. My food happens to be damn good.'

'It's not your fault they can't cook, right?'

'Right.' He nodded emphatically, before a tiny frown appeared between his brows and she could almost hear the cogs turning in his brain. 'What about you? Do you cook any of my recipes?'

'Not really.'

She flipped open the menu, not liking where this thread was heading. She'd hoped Toby's slip-up when they'd first met hadn't registered in all the drama but, by the sly glint in his eyes, she knew he was on to her.

'That's strange, considering Toby recognised me the instant we met because you watched my show all the time.'

Now that his blush had faded and that cheeky grin had returned, she wished she'd never started this. Relaxing was one thing, trying to tease—which bordered on flirting—another.

'Like I said, Marsha's into the whole cooking thing and she often has it on.'

Phew, nice save.

He pinned her with that all-knowing stare of his, the one that said he didn't buy her lousy brush-off for a second, but thankfully let it slide.

'Speaking of cooking, the patisserie is amazing. How do you survive with all the competition in Acland Street?'

She'd asked her parents this very same question when she'd first started in the family business and their motto had stuck: 'quality over quantity, simple is best'. Keeping their legacy going as a successful business was a

dream come true for her. At least, one of her
dreams had come true. Jed had dashed her
other, the one of happily-ever-after, though she
wouldn't go there tonight.

'I stick to making cakes and pastries I do
well. Our range mightn't be as extensive as
other shops in the street but it's the quality that
counts and, thankfully, our customers keep
coming back, not to mention new ones walking
through the door daily.'

She thrived on it: the thrill of baking, creating
mouth-watering temptations, dealing with
people, the whole works. Payet's Patisserie had
a reputation as Melbourne's best and she liked
to keep it that way. Apart from Toby, the
business was her passion, though she had an
awful suspicion that the man sitting opposite
and staring at her as if mesmerised could
quickly join that élite list.

'You really love what you do, don't you?'

He sat forward, appearing to hang on her
every word, and it disconcerted her.

She didn't want to be scrutinised, to be admired.

She wanted answers, starting with the role he intended on playing in Toby's life and why he'd asked her out to dinner.

She may be many things—a distracted mother, a savvy businesswoman, a great pastry chef—but gullible wasn't one of them. This evening had the makings of a date, from the way he'd insisted they dress up to the rapt attention he was paying her. As much as she'd told herself it would be a quick, informal dinner to establish boundaries for parenting Toby, deep down she didn't believe it for a second.

Which brought her back to her earlier question regarding Jed. Why?

For now she'd play it cool but, once she'd demolished one of the grill's huge hamburgers they were famous for, she'd start her inquisition.

'Don't you love your job?'

He nodded. 'Sure, but I don't get the glow you do when you talk about the patisserie. It's great to see someone with that kind of fire.'

Trying not to squirm under his praise—or to think about the type of fire he could light within her given half a chance—she made eye contact with a waiter.

'Ready to order?' she said too brightly, doing a quick scan of the menu to see if her favourite burger was on offer and snapping it shut.

'Why does my admiration make you uncomfortable?'

'That sounds like an interesting name for a burger. I must've missed it on the menu.'

Thankfully, the waiter arrived at that moment and took their orders. However, she should've known he wouldn't let her off that lightly.

'Aimee, look at me.'

'Do I have to? I think the whole cast from my favourite sitcom just walked in the door. And isn't that the lead singer from Spiderbait over there? And—'

'You're scared.'

His quiet, matter-of-fact words drew her attention quicker than if he'd shouted.

'Of what?'

Though she probably already knew the answer and, unfortunately, so did he.

'What's happening between us.'

'There is no us!' Her hand made a move towards her mouth of its own volition and she forced it down with the other under the table. Where was a comforting fingernail to nibble on when she needed it?

He sat back and folded his arms, looking way too smart in his black polo shirt.

She'd always liked him in black and it looked as if he remembered if his appearance tonight was any indication. When she'd first opened her front door and seen him dressed in top-to-toe black, she'd taken a step back in time and experienced the same heart-stopping reaction she had had to him back then.

'You're a smart girl. Do you really need me to spell it out for you?'

She sighed, torn between wanting to fob him off and getting this out in the open. Damn it, she'd wanted to grill him; how had he turned the tables?

'Maybe spending time together for Toby's sake has given you the wrong idea.'

'What idea is that?'

Great, he was going to make her explain when he knew damn well what she was talking about. After all, he'd started down this disastrous track of conversation.

'The idea that there could be something more between us other than as parents to Toby.'

'Oh, *that* idea.' His response could've been humorous, till she glimpsed the serious gleam in his eyes. 'Actually, I think you've got it all wrong.'

Huh?

He obviously took her puzzled silence as an indication to continue. This she had to hear.

'When I said you're scared of what's happening between us, I meant our relating to Toby as parents. I think you're scared of him getting too attached to me. You're scared I'll be the lousy dad you always thought. You're scared I'll botch up my relationship with our son the way I botched up with you.'

Her mouth dropped. Her stomach somersaulted.

How had she got it so wrong?

Of all the embarrassing assumptions to make…she'd thought he was referring to a possible rekindling of their old fire when, in reality, nothing could be further from the truth.

Instead, he'd honed in on all the questions she'd wanted answered in the first place and the reason she'd come tonight. The *only* reason that made sense now that he'd given her the wake-up call she needed.

She could've fluffed her way through an apology for being an ass.

She could've laughed off her ridiculous assumption that he wanted anything more from her than friendship as a co-parent.

Instead, she focused on the one topic guaranteed to get his mind off her humiliating gaffe,

a topic he'd alluded to and she had no intention
of letting him gloss over: the past.

'You did botch up and I could never figure
out why. All your mystery crusades, the times
you bolted out of the apartment after a phone
call from some *distant relative*, the secrets you
used to drive me away at the end. What was
all that about?'

On cue, the shutters came down: his face
blanked of expression, his eyes glazed with
neutrality, his mouth set in a thin line.

Same old, same old, but this time she'd keep
pushing. For Toby's sake, of course. If she
could get to the bottom of why he had walked
away from her, maybe she could prevent history
repeating itself with their son? Toby deserved
more than that, more than what she'd copped.

'It's not relevant. How I treat Toby right now
is what's important.'

'True, but don't you think you owe me an
explanation?'

For a second, she could've sworn she

glimpsed regret in his eyes before it vanished like a whisper of her imagination.

'The past is just that, the past. Let's leave it alone and concentrate on the future, on Toby.'

He was right. What would be the point, pushing him for answers to questions she'd given up pondering a long time ago? She'd loved him, he'd broken her heart. And he didn't think enough of her, even now, to clue her in as to why.

Wuss! Push him! Get the answers you want, the answers you craved for so long before you deluded yourself into believing it didn't matter any more.

Silently telling her voice of reason to shut up, she said, 'Fine. Let's talk about Toby. What are your plans? You heard what Jason said—it could take a year till he's functioning normally again. Are you just sticking around playing some macho version of Florence Nightingale before you vanish, or do you want a permanent part in your son's life? We both know that offer to move in was a knee-jerk reaction to what the doctor said about a stable home environment. Are you ready for the kind of responsibility that being a parent entails? Do you want to be a father for real?'

The questions poured out of her as her voice tightened in anger. She wouldn't lose it. She couldn't. Toby's future depended on Jed's answers and, no matter how furious she was over his avoidance of their past, she had to contain it.

'Honestly? I'm taking it one day at a time.'

Her blood pressure soared at his simple shrug of the shoulders, at his way too simple answer. He might've been able to fob her off but this was her son they were talking about and she wouldn't let up.

'That's a load of bunk and you know it. Giving me some half-baked football coach's cliché won't cut it. You must have some idea of where you see this all going.'

His jaw clenched as he leaned forward, pinning her with a golden stare radiating fire. 'I'm here for Toby like I said I would be when

I first agreed to help. Right now, I haven't got plans to up and leave and I'd like to get to know my son better.'

'But for how long?'

She persisted, sensing she was fighting a losing battle but picking up her weapons and forging ahead anyway.

Nothing had changed. Jed was still the same secretive, closed-off person he'd been at the end of their relationship and it hurt. More than it should.

She'd been a fool for assuming their growing bond had been anything other than two adults supporting each other in a life-threatening situation. Her mum had been right: assume made an ass out of u and me.

'Stop pushing. When I'm ready to leave, I'll let you know.'

When. He'd said *when* he'd leave, not if.

All the confirmation she needed that he had the potential to break Toby's heart the way he had hers.

So what was she going to do about it?

'Here you go, folks. A hamburger and a rib special. Enjoy.'

Giving the waiter a forced smile, she picked up her knife and fork, her appetite vanishing along with her hopes that Jed had changed.

'Look, I don't want us to argue, OK? Let's enjoy the meal.'

'Mmm-hmm,' she mumbled, finding her hamburger infinitely more interesting than making eye contact with him. If she did, her fork might have a sudden urge to make the contact her eyes were avoiding.

'One more thing. The way things ended between us had nothing to do with you. It was my fault.'

Her gaze snapped up at his admission, searching for some sign that he might give her answers to her other questions, answers she suddenly craved.

'You did nothing wrong. I had a choice. I made it, end of story.' He spoke softly, his eyes semi-glazed as if lost in a memory before re-focusing on her, almost pleading. For what? Forgiveness? Acceptance?

Unfortunately for Jed, she was plain out of both but, rather than end the evening in a blazing row before it had started, she sent him a brisk nod and forced a forkful of burger into her mouth.

End of story.

Easy for him to say.

And why, despite his vagueness about the future, did she have a sinking feeling it was only the beginning?

CHAPTER TEN

JED strolled along the St Kilda foreshore, dodging out-of-control roller-bladers and mums with prams while trying to make sense of his predicament. He should've been enjoying the gentle, warm breeze blowing in from Port Phillip Bay, the myriad sailing boats out on a perfect autumn day, the cosmopolitan vibe this funky suburb had to offer.

Instead he trudged along, wishing he could find an easy solution to the countless questions whirling through his head like the crazy bats that flew around here at dusk.

Was he any good at this fatherhood thing or was Toby just clinging to the first male figure in his life since his grandpa died?

Did he want to take a chance on being around on a permanent basis for Toby, guiding him through school, helping him with his homework, taking him to football matches and beyond? Being there for him in the tough teenage years, assisting with career choices, listening to girlfriend problems?

Hell, the mind boggled just thinking about the never-ending responsibility that went with being a dad, a role he'd failed at once before.

And what about Aimee?

When it came to the crunch, he'd chickened out. He'd been contemplating renewing their relationship, seeing if she could forgive him for the past and take a chance on the future. However, her horror at his suggestion to move in had blown that plan out of the water.

Yeah, it had been a spur-of-the-moment thing, the doctor's words about stable home environments and no stress ringing in his ears, and he'd blurted it out without thinking it through, but Aimee's reaction had stunned him none the less. As crazy as it sounded, he thought she might consider it for Toby's sake.

He'd been wrong.

Now he was nervous as hell about pursuing a relationship with Aimee again because this time it wasn't just about them. He had to consider Toby and hurting the little guy wasn't on his agenda. Not now, hopefully not ever.

Try as he might, he couldn't detach his decision-making about Toby from Aimee. She was the boy's mother, part and parcel of what constituted Toby's family, a family he was trying to muscle in on. At least, that was the impression he got from her, the way she had barrelled him up over dinner with all those questions about the future.

As for her probing into their past…he'd been so tempted to tell her the truth, to give her some semblance of reassurance that it hadn't been her fault. In the end he'd given her a snippet, telling her the old 'it's not you, it's me' line and, by the scornful look she'd sent him, she hadn't bought it for a second.

He didn't want her to hurt, to feel guilty about something that had nothing to do with her, but without blurting out the whole sorry tale to her he had no choice.

'Hey, watch it, dude!'

As a speed-freak roller-blader zoomed past, Jed jumped out of the way, twisting his ankle and going down in an undignified heap onto the sand, landing on a flexed wrist that practically groaned under his weight.

Cursing under his breath, he stood up, dusted himself off and tried to move his wrist, wincing at the stabbing pain that shot up his arm. OK, so it wasn't broken but he wouldn't be picking up a ladle or a wok any time soon.

So what's new?

He hadn't been near his restaurant since he'd first come to Melbourne over two months ago and, if he was completely honest, he didn't feel like cooking. For the first time in his life, his

all-consuming passion held no interest, almost
as if the stove-top flame had gone out and a
faulty ignition switch couldn't relight it.

Stress did that to a guy and, unless he got his
act into gear, he'd end up on the scrap heap like
day-old vegetable peel.

His mobile rang and, as he fished it out of his
pocket, he had a sinking feeling he knew who
it would be and a quick scan of the call display
confirmed his fears.

'Hey, Jed. Why haven't you come in to see
your old man?'

'Hi, Dad.'

Damn, why did that word always stick in his
throat? It should roll off his tongue naturally
but somehow, it always felt wrong. A dad
should support you, encourage you, love you
unconditionally, something Larry 'Light-
Fingers' Sanderson had never done.

'So, what's the story, sunshine? Haven't got
time for your dear old dad any more?'

'I've been away on business,' Jed said, not

willing to share the news of his newfound fatherhood with his dad yet.

What for, when the old man would only give him grief just as he had every time they'd talked since his incarceration five years ago?

Jed had supported him through the trial, dealt with the legalities, funded his dad's defence and done everything humanly possible to help his dad through it, including giving up the love of his life. And where had it got him? The old man still treated him like a little kid, trying to boss him around, making light of the serious stuff.

Yet for all Larry's faults, Jed stuck by him, flying up to Brisbane on monthly visits, making him laugh with funny anecdotes from the restaurant, encouraging him to keep the faith.

Simply? He loved his dad, whether Larry deserved it or not, and he'd stopped beating himself up over how stupid he was to feel like this after everything that had happened a long time ago.

'Business? What's so important that you missed your monthly visit again?'

Keeping his voice calm with effort, he said, 'I contacted the prison and let them know I wouldn't be up to see you for a few months. Didn't you get the message?'

'Yeah, but I wanna hear it from you. What's going on? You're not giving me the flick now that I'm due out in a few months, are you?'

Jed clenched the phone and stifled a groan as his sore wrist throbbed. 'If I've stuck by your sorry butt all these years, what makes you think I'll give up on you now?'

He'd thought about it. He'd thought long and hard when the trial was about to start and he'd had to choose between dragging Aimee through the mud—dirty, criminal mud that stuck to anyone unfortunate enough to be associated with Larry—or standing by his dad.

Thankfully, none of the mud had stuck to him due to a journalist's spelling error that gave Larry's surname as Saunderson throughout the trial and, once reported, the spelling had stuck. Not that he'd been famous back then, but once his career took off he'd been grateful for that one little 'u' that protected his anonymity.

Had he been ashamed of his father? Yes.

Had he considered abandoning him? No.

Giving up on his dad had never really been an option, just as he couldn't give up on Toby when Aimee had first approached him for help, even though he hadn't known a thing about the little guy then. For there was one thing his dad had managed to teach him, to instil in him from a young age, and that was the importance of family.

Losing his mum at a young age had bonded the Sanderson men and even his father's regular stints in jail hadn't broken that bond. Jed might be ashamed of his dad, he might resent the choices he'd had to make, but deep down he still loved the old coot. Worse luck.

'Just checking. You still going to get me a job at your restaurant too? I'll be the best damn kitchen-hand you ever had, just wait and see.'

The edge of desperation in his father's voice saddened Jed. They'd gone over their plans following his father's release many times but it looked as if the old man still didn't trust him, after all he'd done.

'Yeah, I know you will. Besides, the boss will kick your butt if you don't work hard.'

'Cheeky whipper-snapper,' Larry said, his gruff voice sounding happier now that he'd badgered Jed to repeat the obvious. 'OK, gotta go. Another lug-head wants to use the phone and my time's up. See ya, son.'

Jed didn't have a chance to respond as the connection terminated abruptly and he flipped the mobile shut and slid it into his pocket.

Son.

He'd tried his damnedest to be the type of son Larry would want and, by the constant reports from the man itself, it still wasn't good enough.

What would Toby think of him if he bailed out after the treatment finished? Would he curse the day he'd ever met his father despite the fact he'd helped save his life?

No doubt about it. He had to take a stand, to make the tough decisions, and right now the only one that made any sense frightened the hell out of him. As for his chances of convincing Aimee to let him become a permanent part of Toby's life, of her life, he didn't have a hope in Hades.

Regardless, he was going to try and give it his best shot.

Aimee had no idea why she'd agreed to meet Jed at the observation deck of the Rialto building. A fitting place actually, high in the sky, right up there with her delusional dreams that Jed had changed.

Dinner the other night had been uncomfortable enough without agreeing to meeting at dusk in one of the most romantic places in Melbourne. She'd wanted answers, he'd given her the old 'it's not you, it's me' line to explain away their past and she hadn't bought it for a second.

Yet here she was, back for more. Spending one-on-one time with Jed wasn't good for her peace of mind. Without Toby acting as a buffer, her nerves were too raw, her feelings too exposed. Having the guy she'd once loved around on a daily basis did that to a girl and she didn't like the vulnerable, helpless feeling he evoked by just being there.

'Thanks for coming.'

She whirled around, annoyed that the deep timbre of Jed's voice had the power to make her pulse race and her heart pound like a jackhammer.

'No problem,' she said, trying not to notice his dark grey designer suit, ivory shirt and funky gold-spotted tie almost the exact colour of his eyes. Eyes that were fixed on her and glowing with repressed excitement.

What did he have to be excited about? Had he reneged on his promise to Toby to stick around, made plans for his return to the high life without them? Wouldn't be the first time he'd changed his mind in a second.

If she'd expected her casual response to dim the feverish light in his eyes she was wrong, as he took a step towards her and tilted her chin up to meet his steady gaze.

'I want to talk about us.'

She gulped, trapped in his gaze like a deer in oncoming headlights, wishing she could look away but powerless to do so. 'I thought we'd already established there is no us.'

'Guess I made a mistake about that.' His thumb moved a fraction, skating across the skin, eliciting an electrifying reaction she tried to ignore. 'We were good together once. This time around, we can be great.'

He'd lost his mind. It was the only explanation that made any sense for his erratic behaviour, shutting her out over dinner, and then pulling this romantic stunt. As for implying they should get back together, he had to be joking. Unfortunately, she didn't feel like laughing.

Wrenching her chin out of his hand and stepping back to establish some much needed physical distance between them, she said, 'There won't be a *this time*. You chose to walk out on me, fine, but this time there's Toby to consider and I won't put him through half of what I went through getting over you.'

'Are you over me?' He spoke softly, his face reflecting regret.

'I have to be, for my sake and Toby's,' she murmured, annoyed that her voice wavered as the painful memory of losing Jed washed over her.

She hadn't meant to be that honest. She'd been battling hard over the last few weeks, maintaining a tight grip on her emotions, trying not to let Jed's natural warmth draw her back in. It had been tough and in the end useless as she finally acknowledged the painful truth: having Jed back in her life felt good, way too good, and resurrected a host of feelings she'd be better off forgetting.

How stupid could she be, starting to have feelings for the guy who'd thrown her love back in her face five years ago? She'd scorned women who never learned from their mistakes, who went back to abusive partners, who slipped into victim mode like a second skin. Yet here she was, a glutton for punishment, falling into the same old trap of wishing for something that just couldn't be.

'That's not a straight answer.'

'You have the audacity to ask me for a straight answer? You, the king of deception?'

Her remark hit home as the glow faded from his eyes and he shook his head. 'Just this once, do you think you could put your resentment of the past behind and give me a break?'

Why should I? You hurt me! She wanted to scream. Instead, she schooled her features into a bland mask and asked, 'Where's all this coming from? Why are we here?'

'Because we need to talk.'

Yep, Jed was definitely leaving. First the old 'it's me, not you' line the other night, now the 'we need to talk' stinker. Couldn't he just get it over and done with? It's not as if she hadn't had to cope with a walk-out by him before, though pain gripped her heart at how she'd comfort Toby.

Taking her mutinous silence as agreement, he continued. 'You know how you didn't trust me to be a part of Toby's life for the first five years, thinking I'd make a lousy dad?'

'Look, I—'

'You were probably right. It's taken me a while to figure out I'm not half bad at the whole parenting thing and, what's more, I like it.'

'You have been great with Toby.'

She'd give him that much, and seeing how good he was with their son had pierced her with guilt on a daily basis.

Maybe she had made the wrong decision in keeping Jed from Toby? Sure, she couldn't have contacted him initially while recovering from her broken heart but, once she'd got a grip on her emotions, she could have told him, could have given him the opportunity to be a dad.

He was right. She'd robbed him of the first

five years of Toby's life, those precious formative years he'd never get back, and it made her feel awful.

'Thanks,' he said. 'And I intend on keeping up my fantastic father skills. Long-term, if you'll agree. Now, why don't you open this?'

Her heart stopped as he pulled a small square box from his pocket, opened it and held it out to her, a smile as wide as Port Phillip Bay on his face.

'No way,' she said, her heart restarting with a resounding thud before racing ahead of itself as she stared in amazement at the stunning princess-cut diamond nestled in white gold.

'Mmm…not quite the response I hoped for but I guess we can work on it.' He pulled the exquisite ring from the box and reached for her left hand. 'Aimee, will you marry me? I want us to be a family, to be the kind of family that Toby deserves.'

This couldn't be happening…

Five years ago she would have jumped up and down on the spot, shoved that ring on her finger and flung her arms around his neck, screaming 'yes' from the top of the tallest peak on Dunk Island to the widest stretch of sandy beach.

Five years ago she'd dreamed of a proposal, expected a proposal, and soon learned that life didn't live up to expectations.

Yet here Jed was, doing all the right things, saying all the right things, yet it was all wrong.

And, as the fog of shock cleared at his spontaneous gesture, reality intruded, sharpening previously blurred edges till she wondered how she could've been so blind.

Jed didn't want her, he wanted Toby.

He'd said as much, his proposal talking about family, not about love. In fact, he'd gone out of his way over dinner to clear up any misconceptions she might have regarding his feelings for her, driving the point home in no uncertain terms.

Yet for one brief, heart-stopping moment,

she'd almost believed in dreams again. And hated herself for it.

'No!'

She snatched her hand away and tucked it under her opposite elbow, where he couldn't get at it.

Jed gaped and the ring fell with a soft plop onto the carpet beneath their feet, bouncing till it lay a foot away, twinkling up at them in the muted light.

She wrenched her gaze away from its sparkling beauty and focused on saying what should have been said a long time ago.

'You want to be a family? Well, let me tell you something about families. Families trust each other, they depend on each other, they open up and laugh and cry together. In a nutshell, they're honest with each other and I don't think you've been honest with me, have you, Jed?'

His quick glance away confirmed his guilt and her heart shattered completely. If he'd denied it, opened up to her, given her some semblance of truth now, when she needed it most, they might have had a chance. Instead, a dull flush stained his tanned cheeks as she continued.

'I still have no idea what you were hiding five years ago or what continues to haunt you, to drive a wedge between us. What's worse, you have no intention of telling me. You expect me to take the little morsels of affection you throw my way and be grateful for it. Grateful enough to *marry* you?' The words poured out of her mouth, bitter words, angry words but, best of all, the truth. 'You talk about being a family? Well, I've got a newsflash for you. Families are based on love. One hundred per cent unconditional love, and that's something we don't have.'

'But what about Toby? The doc said the first year post-transplant is critical for recovery. He can't be stressed by emotional stuff.'

'We've already been through all this with that stupid idea you had to move in. Didn't you hear me the first time when I said it wouldn't happen? What did you think—giving me a fancy ring and some lousy proposal would change all that?'

If her heart had shattered a moment ago, it now fragmented and stabbed through her body, eliciting such intense pain that she almost doubled over.

'We need to do this. For Toby's sake.' He grabbed her hand before she had a chance to react and her defence mechanisms kicked in. Icy cold dread flowed through her veins at what she'd have to go through all over again to get over Jed if she let herself be swept away by his proposal, even for Toby's sake, and she knew she needed to flee before she fell apart.

Taking a steadying breath and blinking back the tears that threatened to overflow, she said, *'For Toby's sake*, I'll pretend this never happened. You can still drop by the apartment, spend as much time as you want with him and I'll try to forget you put me in this position. That way, you can still be a father for Toby. You'll get what you want and everyone will be happy.' Except her. The devastation of always being second-best to Jed would haunt her for the rest of her life. 'Just don't push me.'

Pain ripped across his face, ageing him ten years before her eyes. 'I don't want it to be like this. I want us all to be together.'

For a horrifying second, she thought he might cry as his voice shook and a sheen glazed his eyes. At least she could be reassured by the depth of his feelings for Toby. He wanted to give his son a family so much he'd enter into a loveless marriage to do so.

Dashing a hand over her eyes as the tears spilled over and trickled down her cheeks, she forced herself to meet his gaze. 'I know what you think you want. The thing is, we don't always get it.'

Summoning every ounce of courage she possessed, she walked towards the lift, into the steel-enclosed cubicle and closed her eyes as the doors slid shut, determined not to look back.

To never look back.

CHAPTER ELEVEN

JED clasped Toby's small hand in his, enjoying the contact as they strolled along the esplanade on a busy Sunday morning while trying to avert his gaze from Aimee.

He'd botched up. Big time.

If he'd thought his proposal might give her the reassurance she seemed to crave about his intentions to stay around, he'd been wrong. He'd had it all planned out: take her to the potential site for his new restaurant in Melbourne, discuss his plans for the future, *their* future, and come clean about his dad and why he'd done what he had in the past.

Instead, he'd mucked up the execution from whoa to go, getting all tangled up in trying to express how much she meant to him without sounding corny, trying to ascertain whether she still had any feelings for him at all. Then her fervent refusal had shocked him into silence, followed by a huge back-pedal that left him floundering like a teenager with his first girl-friend. Fearing all was lost, he'd started bumbling on about Toby, hoping to play on her love for her son in order to give him a chance.

Bad move.

Catastrophic move.

And in that instant when she'd looked at him with devastation in her eyes, it had hit him like a cast-iron frying-pan on the head.

He loved her. He loved their son.

A huge, overwhelming, terrifying love that had him shaking down to his soul.

If he was completely honest with himself, he'd always loved Aimee, had never stopped loving her, and spending time with her even in the tough times they'd faced in the acute phase of Toby's treatment had reinforced that love. As for Toby, he wanted to be a father to the little boy, he wanted a chance to try. More than he'd ever wanted anything in his life.

Apart from a second chance with Aimee, that was.

But he wasn't a fool. She'd said not to push her and he'd listened. He knew he had a long way to go to prove how he felt, to convince her he wasn't some idiot only intent on marrying her for Toby's sake. Lucky for him, she hadn't shut him out or avoided him since the disastrous proposal last week. Instead, she maintained a polite, friendly veneer, probably for Toby's benefit, but he'd seen the vulnerability in her eyes the few times he'd caught her unawares and it hurt him. It near killed him, but he'd botched up badly once; he wouldn't do it again. This time, he'd take it slow and hope she'd take a chance on a fool like him.

'Are you tired yet, sweetheart?' Aimee stopped strolling and bent down to eye level with Toby.

'I'm fine, Mum.' Toby rolled his eyes and looked up at Jed for support. 'Tell her, Dad.'

Jed squatted down too and tweaked Toby's nose. 'Your mum's just looking out for you.' Something he should be doing for both of them and would if she gave him a chance. 'This is your first outing and we don't want to overdo it.'

'Yeah, OK.' Toby pouted for a second before spying his favourite ice-cream shop. 'Actually, I am a bit tired. Can I rest over there?'

'With a chocolate ice in your hand, perhaps?' Aimee said, laughing at the surprised expression on Toby's face that she was on to him.

With his cleverness, she sometimes forgot her son was just a regular kid, trying the same stunts and pulling the same tricks that kids did the world over.

'Sounds cool to me,' Toby said, tugging on her hand and Jed's at the same time. 'Let's go.'

As they strolled towards the ice cream shop, Aimee tried to ignore the feeling of contentment that ambling along the esplanade on a lazy Sunday morning with Toby between her and Jed could bring. For all intents and purposes, they felt like a real family and looked like countless other families browsing through the market stalls.

However, they weren't a real family and, after Jed's appalling proposal last week, they never would be. He hadn't had the decency to mention feelings or possibly clear up their messy past. Uh-uh. Instead he'd tried to placate her with that gorgeous ring, to play on her love for her son to ensure he had a permanent role in Toby's life.

What was wrong with the guy? Would he go to any lengths to secure a place in Toby's heart? Well, she had news for him. He didn't need to try so hard or go to such desperate measures as to marry her, a woman he obviously had little regard for let alone loved.

If he felt one tenth of what she did for him, he wouldn't have put her through that farcical proposal. He would have sat her down, ex-plained his mysterious past and offered her a chance at rekindling what they had once had, perhaps seeing where the possibility of a relationship might take them.

Instead he'd made her feel a fool to contemplate a possible reunion, though, try as she might, she still couldn't quell the buzz that zapped through her body whenever she saw him.

Like today. The guy wore khaki shorts, a white T-shirt and deck shoes. Not remarkable in itself but throw in a pair of long, lean legs in those shorts and a broad, muscular chest in the T-shirt and her hormones were doing a happy dance.

Not good.

Besides, she didn't acknowledge her hormones any more. Look what had happened the last time she had: she'd fallen in love, had her heart trampled on and fallen pregnant. Though, glancing down at Toby and the way the sun streaked through his blond hair, how he finally had some colour back in his cheeks and the simple mechanical action of him putting one foot in front of the other after resting inside for so long, she didn't blame her hormones one bit.

Being in love with Jed years ago mightn't have been good for her but the joy she took in her son more than made up for it every day.

'Would you like an ice cream?' Jed asked as they neared the shop, reaching into his pocket for his wallet.

At least she couldn't fault him there. Though she hadn't needed or asked for his financial assistance, he'd insisted on paying Toby's medical bills and had showered him with gifts to keep his spirits high while confined to bed. Initially she'd been angry, equating his blatant splashing of cash as a way to buy Toby's affection, but seeing them together with his gifts, having fun for hours, had allayed her fears.

Besides, what was she so afraid of? It wasn't as if Jed could buy his way into Toby's heart. Her little boy was way too smart for that.

'I'd love a scoop of mango and a scoop of lemon, in a cup, please,' she said, suddenly in need of something icy cold to douse the heat flooding her body at his intense stare.

She must be nuts. How could a simple question regarding ice cream send her into a spin?

OK, so Jed had a goofy smile on his face and enough warmth radiating from his eyes to heat her ten times over, but it didn't *mean* anything. He was just being friendly, for goodness' sake! Maintaining the nice, civilised façade they'd slipped into since that awful night at the Rialto for Toby's sake.

'I remember that sweet tooth of yours,' Jed said, dropping his voice intimately low, instantly creating the impression they were the only two people in the world.

'And I'll have a chocolate one in a cone!'

Toby's shout shattered her silly illusion and she stopped herself from physically shaking her head to dispel her weird mood.

Aimee plus Toby plus Jed did *not* equal happily-ever-after.

Today was about Toby. Everything they'd

done together over the last few months had been about Toby and she really needed to drum it into her fanciful head.

So what if the three of them together felt natural?

So what if they'd spent almost every moment of the last few months together?

So what if Jed had done way more than she'd expected or would have given him credit for, putting his life on hold for them?

It didn't mean the warmth he aroused in her was anything more than gratitude.

Yeah, that was it. She was grateful. Very grateful. So grateful that she'd lost her grip on reality and made an absolute fool of herself in assuming there was more going on between them than this: two people with a past, trying to create a present for their one common bond.

As for Toby's future, she'd given up badgering him. She'd played it straight and hard, and look where that had got her: an empty proposal and a bruised ego for her trouble.

'Did I hear you say the P word?' Jed tried a mock frown, which ended up looking like a clown's smirk, and she stifled a giggle.

For a guy who reportedly didn't have the faintest idea about being a dad, he was doing a mighty fine job.

Suitably chastised, Toby said, 'Can I please have a chocolate cone?'

'You sure can.' Jed ruffled his hair and turned to the young girl behind the counter to place their order.

Not a good move, considering it gave her an unimpeded view of the back of those rather ordinary khaki shorts filled out by a rather extraordinary butt.

Oh, boy.

'Here you go.'

Unfortunately, Jed turned a fraction too quickly and she didn't react fast enough, her gaze meeting his a moment too late. By the devilish glint in his eyes, he knew exactly what she'd been staring at. Drat the man!

'Thanks.' At least her voice didn't waver but her cool act was foiled by his fingers brushing hers as he handed over the cup filled with mouth-watering sorbet, causing her hand to shake and almost drop the lot.

'You OK?' Far from him being concerned, a wide grin had joined the knowing glint in his eyes and she nodded, plopped down in the nearest seat and concentrated on devouring her sorbet without tipping the contents over her favourite denim skirt and red peasant top.

Sheesh, her behaviour was too embarrassing for words and, hot on the heels of her adamant refusal of his proposal, made her look like a wavering bimbo.

Maybe she had a case of kidnapper-hostage misplaced affection, where the hostage spent so much time with the kidnapper that they went a bit bonkers and started to actually like their kidnapper.

Yeah, that would explain it. She and Jed had been forced into spending close company over the last few months and her weird lust for the guy must stem from that. It had to. She wouldn't contemplate any other explanation.

Unfortunately, when she'd first approached Jed for help she hadn't banked on any of this happening. She'd prayed he'd be compatible, hoped he'd donate and assumed he'd get out of their lives pronto, ditching them faster than he'd ditched her five years earlier.

She'd never dreamed they'd be doing stuff like this together: family stuff, couple stuff. Stuff that twisted her insides into tighter knots than the ones she created for the tops of her cherry lattice pies.

Besides, she didn't even like the guy. He'd broken her heart and hadn't looked back. How could she even entertain the thought of taking their friendship further, right after his dud proposal?

Maybe you never stopped loving him?

And maybe she'd had a brain transplant alongside Toby's bone marrow one!

Of all the stupid ideas…

She'd given up on love when Jed had discarded her like yesterday's leftovers and no way, no how could she label her current feelings towards him as anything remotely like the head-over-heels dummy she'd been back then.

Respect. Yeah, that was what she felt for him now. He'd done the right thing by Toby and she respected him for it.

Then why the buzz?

Hormones. Chemistry. Just because she didn't sample every pastry in her shop didn't mean she couldn't look. And drool...

'This is so yummy,' Toby said, running his tongue around the rim of his cone to lap up the fast-melting drips.

'Sure is,' Jed said, doing something similar to his double peppermint-choc-chip.

However, when Jed did it a sizzle of heat shot through her and she glanced away quickly, suddenly fascinated by a tram trundling past.

No matter how she explained it, made excuses for it or tried to ignore it, she knew she had *it* bad!

Shovelling the last of the sorbet into her mouth in record time, she leaped to her feet and deposited the cup in a nearby bin. 'How about I leave you guys here for a minute while I check out that stall over there?'

'Oh-oh.' Toby groaned and rolled his eyes.

'What's up?' Jed's head swivelled between them, totally lost as she playfully tweaked Toby's nose.

'Mum always spends ages looking at the necklaces and stuff. It's boring.'

'But we spend time looking at the kites too,' she said, enjoying the banter with her son, who hadn't been to St Kilda's famous Sunday esplanade market in months. 'Maybe we shouldn't look at anything and just go home?'

Jed's impressed gaze read 'nasty but smart move' and she winked, knowing Toby's response before he opened his chocolate-covered mouth.

'That's OK, Mum. Me and Dad will stay here while you look at all your stuff and then we'll look at the kites.'

'Good idea, champ. We'll talk about boy stuff while your mum browses.'

Flashing Jed a grateful smile, she walked away, trying to keep to a sedate pace rather than the full-on sprint she wanted to do.

Space. She needed space away from Jed to get her weird hormones under control, even if she only had a few minutes' reprieve.

However, browsing through the stalls she usually loved didn't bring the peace she'd anticipated, as every time she glanced over at Toby Jed's gaze locked on hers, packing a powerful punch even at a distance.

What was wrong with her? No matter how much he'd hurt her with that meaningless proposal, she couldn't shake off the closeness they'd forged over the last few months with Toby. She liked him, genuinely liked him, and despite the two blatant blots on his copybook, the throw-away moving-in thing and the proposal from hell, she couldn't harden her heart enough not to care.

Somehow, in refusing Jed and hoping to create an emotional distance between them, he'd become more attractive to her.

She strolled past several stalls selling abstract art, Australiana souvenirs and hand-made soaps, determinedly not looking Jed's way.

Of course, her little plan to ignore him for a few minutes came totally undone when the man himself sneaked up on her while she was examining a delicate silver necklace with a stunning silver swirl pendant.

'That would look great on you,' he said, his breath fanning her ear and sending a shiver down her spine.

Thankfully, Toby's insistent tugging on her skirt saved her from answering.

'Is it time to look at the kites yet?'

Laying down the necklace, she smiled her thanks at the stall-holder and bent down to Toby. 'You sure you're not too tired?'

'Mum!'

She chuckled. 'OK. Let's go, but after we check out the kites it's home time. Deal?'

'Deal,' Toby said, his eyes already drawn to the brightly coloured display at the end of the row.

As Toby walked a few paces in front of them, Jed fell into step next to her and she stared straight ahead, unwilling to give her crazy hormones a chance to do any more damage.

'Do you remember the yin and yang necklace I gave you?'

'Uh-huh,' she said, instantly transported back to the night of their first anniversary. He'd cooked her Beef Wellington and chocolate pudding, given her the yin half of the necklace while keeping the yang half for himself, saying they were two halves of a whole before making love to her all night long.

Those were the days, she thought, before mentally slapping herself for heading down that track.

'Do you still have it?'

'What do you think?' she snapped, finding this trip down memory lane disturbing.

For a guy who wouldn't give her a straight answer about the past, he had no right dredging up something as special and romantic as an anniversary, nor a gift that held such significance for them both.

He stared at her, his eyes unreadable as he slid sunglasses into place before shrugging and picking up the pace again. 'Yeah, as if. Come on. We've got a date with a kite salesman,' he said, joining Toby and leaving her with an ache in the vicinity of her heart.

Yeah, as if.

Holding on to a necklace like that would mean she still valued its significance and still held a special place in her heart for the guy who'd given it to her.

It could even mean she'd always loved that guy, no matter how much he'd hurt her.

Or perhaps it meant she was a sentimental

fool, hanging on to a piece of the past for old times' sake.

Right now, she didn't want to delve into the reasons why she'd kept the necklace or why her yin might have taken a whole new shine to his yang.

CHAPTER TWELVE

JED had analysed, dissected and pondered every moment of the last few weeks with Aimee and, whichever way he looked at it, he was no closer to discovering if she felt anything more than grudging respect for him.

One minute she was the polite friend, the next—like that day at the esplanade—she'd looked ready to gobble him up. Accepting he had a son had been scary but figuring out Aimee and reading her mood swings was downright terrifying.

The funny thing was, he'd tried to forget her over the years by dating women the antithesis of her, by throwing himself into his work and, most importantly, by keeping strong ties to the man he'd given her up for in the first place.

None of it had worked and all it had taken was a few months in her addictive company to make him crave her even more.

Did they have a chance together? Damned if he knew, but one thing was for certain; tonight would be another step in finding out.

'You're crazy,' Aimee said, smiling up at him as they waited patiently in the long queue for the Mad Mouse at Luna Park.

'Toby insisted I try out his favourite roller coaster and see if it still works,' he said, hoping he could keep that special smile on her face for the whole evening.

Nobody smiled like Aimee, her whole face lighting up and her eyes exuding a warmth that beckoned like an open fire on a cold winter's day.

He'd missed her so much, more than he'd let himself believe. But then, the Sanderson men were big on self-delusion.

'Yeah, well, he asked me to keep an eye on you and tell him if you screamed or threw up.'

'My son doesn't have much faith in me, does he?'

'He has enough,' she said, touching his arm for a second before turning away quickly, as if embarrassed by her show of reassurance.

He chuckled and draped an arm over her shoulders, hoping she wouldn't shrug it off, feeling a million bucks when she didn't.

'Really? Well, guess what? He said the same to me about you.'

Though she'd initially stiffened when he'd draped his arm over her, she relaxed as she joined in his laughter. 'That cheeky brat.'

'Yeah, but cute. Marsha's going to have her hands full tonight, now that he's getting so much energy back.'

'She's used to it. Toby's been full-on the last few years since my folks died and if it wasn't for her I'd never have been able to keep the patisserie open and be a single parent.'

A shaft of guilt pierced him that he hadn't been around to lend a hand. Then again, would he have wanted to? He'd been wrapped up in his dad's messy life—would he have been mature enough to handle raising Toby too? He doubted it.

'Must've been tough,' he said, not wanting to dwell on how much of a loser she must have thought he was not to involve him in parenting Toby.

She shrugged and managed to dislodge his arm in the process, a smooth move that rode roughshod over his hopes.

'We managed. Though Marsha has really come to the fore these last few months. What with managing the shop and helping with the baking, she's a whizz.'

'Hey, you're a whizz too. You've been the one getting up at four every morning to fill those tantalising windows before rushing to the hospital and back. Throw in the overall man-agement of the place, the banking and playing nurse to one demanding kid and you've got the makings of a saint.'

She shifted her weight from one foot to the other, uncomfortable under his praise. 'And what does that make you? The devil? You've done your fair share of helping out.' She lifted her hand as if to count off his good points on her fingers and he noticed she'd started to grow her nails, something she'd tried to do in the past but she always ended up nibbling on them when nervous.

So much for hoping she might have feelings for him. If that were the case, he knew her nails would be chewed to the quick.

'Let's see. You've donated marrow, redecorated Toby's room, played endless hands of snap, read him bedtime stories and stuck around.' She paused, biting on her bottom lip, and he had the sudden urge to do the same, damn the consequences. 'In my book, that puts you right up there next to me in the halo stakes.'

'In that case, do I get a reward?' he murmured, spurred on by the admiration written all over her beautiful face. The face he wanted to cradle between his hands, the face he'd once showered with kisses and yearned to again.

Her pupils dilated and her glossed lips parted as she registered his meaning while her body swayed a fraction towards him, giving him all the incentive he needed.

He had to kiss her. He *needed* to kiss her.

However, as he closed the short distance between them, a loud voice intruded.

'Tickets, please!' and they jumped apart like oil and water in a sizzling pan.

'He's got them,' she said, flashing the teenage ticket collector a bright smile before ducking through the turnstile and sending him a saucy wave.

Shaking his head at the guy's lousy timing— and his poor form that their first kiss in five years would have taken place in front of a crowd waiting for some kiddie roller coaster—he fumbled in his pockets for the tickets, handed them over and followed Aimee. He hadn't pushed her since his bombed proposal, taking it nice and slow, but somehow, tonight had changed all that. He was through playing tortoise. Time to give the hare a go and, hopefully, they'd all get to cross the winning line together.

It had been a magical night. Aimee couldn't remember the last time she'd been this relaxed.

Or her body this hyped.

Every time Jed brushed against her, electricity skittered across her skin as if she'd been zapped.

Every time Jed smiled at her, her stomach did a good impersonation of an apple turnover—though the turning over part happened so many times, she felt sick.

As for that almost-kiss a few hours ago, her wobbly legs still hadn't recovered.

This shouldn't be happening. She shouldn't be feeling this disoriented, this electrified, as if the slightest spark would set her off and launching straight in Jed's direction.

What had happened to not trusting the guy?

To all the secrets he harboured? To the way he'd treated her in the past? In the present?

All of it faded into oblivion every time he stared at her with those hypnotic golden eyes or smiled that sexy grin designed just for her.

Oh, boy.

'This festival is something else,' he said, balancing a hot dog in one hand and a cola in the other as they fought their way through the crowd towards a recently vacated bench overlooking the bay.

'Sure is. I love living in St Kilda. The beach on our doorstep, the most eclectic mix of people and restaurants in Melbourne and this.'

She threw her arms wide, encompassing the funky bands vying for space alongside talented buskers, the trendy crowd happily jostling along Acland St and spilling out onto the esplanade, the majestic Palais theatre, where she'd seen some of the coolest acts in Australia.

Living here was the best, but then, sharing an apartment with Jed on Dunk Island had been pretty special too. More than special, it had been her dream. Before he had turned it into a nightmare.

'You know what I love?' he said, laying down his food and drink on the bench and turning towards her as her heart stalled, skipped and re-started again at a frantic pace.

'What?'

Surely that soft, breathy voice hadn't come from her? She'd never spoken like that in her life and now was a heck of a time to start, what with the guy she'd never got over looking at her as if she were the world's tastiest pavlova and he was about to take a big bite.

'I love how you can still love life after every-thing you've been through.'

He reached for her hand and she let him hold it, even though his thumb brushing the back of it sent heat slamming through her body, thawing the icy shield around her heart. 'Losing your parents, Toby's illness. Us.'

She almost missed the last word and leaned

forward to catch it, a bad move if she didn't want to give him the wrong idea, a good move if she wanted to satisfy her curiosity that he still kissed the same, tasted the same.

As his lips met hers, warm, firm, demanding, and she melted into him like marshmallows in hot chocolate, she knew without a doubt it had been a great move.

The years apart fell away as he kissed her, a frantic, hungry kiss that soon gave way to slow, sensual mastery. Her hands tangled in his hair, pulling him closer, starving for more. He obliged, scattering feather-light kisses over her face, her jaw, even the tip of her nose before re-claiming her mouth, sending her into orbit.

He kissed the same, yet different.

Back then, had she been this overwhelmed, this shaken? Yes, he was sexy and yes, he turned her on, but as he deepened his kiss, his tongue teasing her to join him in its pleasure game, she knew this soul-deep attraction was more than physical.

And it scared her to death.

He broke away first, staring at her with a dazed look that made her want to reach out and do it all over again, afraid or not. His eyes glowed amber in the soft streetlight and, if she hadn't known any better, the tender expression in them exactly matched how he'd once looked at her. Every time he'd told her he loved her, in fact, and that had been often.

'Nights like this make me do crazy things,' he said, sending her a half-sheepish, half-apologetic smile before looking away and staring at the shimmering water dotted with lights from the marina near by.

'Nights like what?'

Thankful he'd broken the awkward post-kiss silence first, she studied his profile: the straight nose, the strong chin, the impressive cheek-bones, wondering if Toby would grow up to be as handsome as his father.

'Nights filled with music and laughter and people having fun. Nights like this give me a buzz.'

'Me too,' she said, needing any excuse to explain her crazy behaviour in letting him kiss her like a maniac in public and gratefully latching on to his.

Jed was half right. Tonight had given her a buzz and it had nothing to do with the festival. Being with him, chatting, flirting, reconnecting in a way that had her mind, not to mention her heart, reeling; now, that was a buzz.

'Want to take a walk on the pier?'

No, she wanted some answers, the primary one being why he'd really kissed her. They'd been dancing around one another all night—if she was completely honest, for several weeks now. The tension had been building and, as much as she'd chastised herself for it being all in her own head, it looked as if he'd been feeling it too.

'OK.' She stood up, torn between wanting to dash across the few hundred metres to her home and hiding, and staying out all night despite the possible reaction of her traitorous body. 'What about your food?'

'I'm not hungry.' He deposited the hot dog and cola can in a nearby bin, thrust his hands in his pockets and started walking.

O-K. So much for romance. If she'd expected a little hand-holding after their mind-blowing kiss, she'd been sorely mistaken.

Falling into step beside him, she wondered if they'd ever deal with their past, knowing it needed to happen if they were to have a future.

Reaching the end of the pier, she took a deep breath and took the plunge, so to speak. 'That kiss wasn't just about the night vibe, was it?'

He turned, a tortured look flitting across his face in the moonlight, a look that didn't bode well for the long-awaited exchanging of home-truths.

'No, it wasn't.'

She waited for more but, like the time of his farewell speech five years earlier, he just stood there, regret and sadness turning his eyes dark caramel, his lips compressed in an 'I'm not telling' line.

'This is a waste of time,' she muttered, swivelling on her heel and heading for the shore.

'Wait!'

But Aimee didn't. Instead she picked up her feet, grateful for the flat sandals she'd worn, and ran down the pier, her shoes making hollow, thumping sounds against the ancient wood, similar sounds to her heart.

Now wasn't the time to hear Jed's home-truths. How could she, when a staggering home-truth of her own had suddenly flared to life, leaving her more vulnerable than ever?

The tension, the build-up, the kiss; it had all been part of an emotion she'd wanted to avoid at all costs, an emotion she'd shut down the minute Jed had walked out of their apartment and never come back.

She could dress it up, make all the excuses in the world or run the way she was doing at the moment, but nothing could stop her from realising the awful truth.

She loved Jed.

Always had, probably always would.

And with their past lying between them like an old, festering wound, there wasn't one darn thing she could do about it.

CHAPTER THIRTEEN

'HAVE you ever flown a kite before, Dad?'

Toby looked up at Jed, glowing with excitement.

'No, I didn't have a kite when I was a kid.' *I didn't have a father when I was a kid, not a real one, anyway.* 'You'll have to show me how to do it.'

'No worries.'

Jed watched Toby lay the kite on the grass, check the strings and do some weird thing where he licked his finger and held it up in the air.

'Just checking the wind, Dad. It's an important part of kite flying.'

'Lucky I've got you to show me the ropes,' Jed said, his heart close to bursting at the earnest look on Toby's face as he got the kite airborne and the ear-splitting smile as it stayed up there.

Toby's intelligence staggered him. And scared him. What would he know about algebra and logarithms and all that other stuff when the time came? His forte was sautéing and fricasseeing, though he guessed he'd adapt. He'd do catch-up classes if it meant sharing a slice of his son's life.

'Wanna turn?'

'Sure.'

Toby gave Jed the handle and he pretended to struggle. 'Think you could lend me a hand here? I'm having a bit of trouble.'

'OK.'

Toby placed his small hand over Jed's and they controlled the giant Batman kite with ease.

With the sun beating down, a brisk breeze off the bay and his son's hand clasping his, contentment wrapped Jed in a warm cocoon that he never wanted to shrug off.

This was what life was about, precious

moments of unconditional love that couldn't be replicated or bought no matter how much money you had or how famous you were.

And to think he'd been shying away from this at the start, too scared to take a chance again.

'Dad, can I ask you something?'

'Sure. Shoot.'

'When I'm all better, do you think you'll still want to play with me?'

Jed's heart stuttered before kick-starting again. Hell, had his plan to woo Aimee slowly wrought more havoc than he'd thought? He'd thought it was the right thing to do but Toby's question, softly spoken with a hint of desperation, shattered him. What had he done?

'Listen up.' He pulled Toby onto his squatted knee, their hands still joined on the handle, their faces inches apart. 'I know I wasn't around for a long time but, now that I'm here, I'm not leaving. I haven't been sticking around because you're sick, I'm sticking around because I love you and you're a great kid.

You're *my* kid and I'm going to be your dad and we're going to live happily ever after, just like all those stories say, OK?'

'Cool!' Toby's wide grin matched his own and as they stayed in that position, son perched on father's knee, hands joined, Jed knew that time was running out.

He needed to up the ante with Aimee despite his renewed intentions to take things slowly after that scintillating kiss they'd shared last night.

She'd mistaken his reticence afterwards as a sign he wasn't interested, when nothing was further from the truth. He'd had to keep his distance, to keep his hands off her, otherwise his plan to woo her slowly would have been blown sky-high.

He'd been a mess all evening, trying not to drool as her flirty floral dress swished around her knees or dipped low in the front when she bent forward to eat her fairy floss, trying to keep from hauling her into his arms and never letting go.

Then the kiss happened and he'd had to pull back, establish some distance before he blew it, big time. Again.

But she'd run before he'd had a chance to explain, before he could set things right between them.

Now he couldn't wait any longer.

Toby's anxiety had put paid to that plan. He needed to tell Aimee the truth, to come clean about everything and hope to God she had it in her heart to forgive him.

And to love him.

'Time to wash for dinner, Tobes.'

Aimee carefully removed a roast lamb from the oven and laid it on the stove top, inhaling the rich aroma of sizzling meat, rosemary and garlic.

'OK, Mum. But I get some of the outside crunchy bits, right?'

'Right,' she said, thankful that Toby's appetite had finally returned. They might not be out of the woods completely but, months down the track since his marrow transplant, his colour had returned, his strength wasn't far behind and his hospital visits had dwindled.

All in all, life was good.

'That's some roast.' Jed joined her at the bench top, picking up a huge knife and fork for carving duties.

'Even if you do say so yourself. Though lamb always was your speciality, wasn't it?'

He studied her for a moment as if checking for hidden barbs in her comment, before replying.

'Sure, and it's still a favourite.'

His hesitation before answering wasn't reassuring. She thought they'd passed the uncomfortable stage ages ago but, since that kiss last night, he'd been tiptoeing on eggshells around her.

Not that he had anything to worry about. After all, he wasn't the idiot who'd gone and fallen in love a second time around.

'You'll have to show me your secret. That way, I can do a roast every week and impress whoever drops by.'

He sent her a puzzled stare and she chuckled. 'Well, you never know your luck in a big city.'

'You're in a strange mood tonight.' He started carving the meat, sending her sideways glances as she arranged roasted vegetables on three plates beside him. 'I'm not sure if you're having a go at me or just trying to be funny.'

Honestly? She didn't know herself. Being around Jed, having him here, doing family stuff together was becoming increasingly difficult. The closer he got to Toby, the happier she should be.

Instead, since that kiss and the stunning realisation she'd fallen for him, she didn't know how to act or what to say any more. Where they'd developed an easy-going camaraderie over the last few months, despite a few disastrous hiccups on the way, an invisible wall had been erected recently and she had no idea how to break it down. Or if she truly wanted to.

Maybe it was for the best. Distance herself

emotionally from him, continue being his friend, make sure he did right by Toby. Easy, right?

'Wow, that smells awesome!' Toby bounced into the kitchen and Aimee smiled, relieved at the interruption and genuinely happy to see her son acting like his old self.

'We'll finish this chat later,' Jed murmured, serving meat onto the plates and ladling gravy over the lot, while she pretended not to hear him as she whizzed the plates out from under him and placed them on the table.

'Did Dad tell you his news?' Toby forked pumpkin and potato into his mouth, looking at her expectantly.

Her heart stilled for a second. Surely Jed hadn't discussed leaving with Toby before her?

'What news?' She managed to sound casual, though the white knuckles as she clenched her cutlery must have been a dead giveaway as Jed raised an eyebrow in her direction.

'Dad's sticking around. Isn't that great?' Another forkful of roast and beans followed the first and she could barely make out what Toby had said. But she'd got the general gist.

How dared Jed go ahead and tell Toby something like that when they hadn't discussed the major issues, like access visits and the legalities?

'Yeah, great,' she said, managing a tight smile for Toby's benefit while sending Jed a cold glare designed to intimidate.

By his answering grin, it didn't work.

'It's going to be so cool having my dad around,' Toby said, continuing to shovel food into his mouth at an alarming rate. 'We can go sailing and roller-blading and kite flying all the time!'

'Don't forget you're starting school next year,' she said, sounding like a drip and hating herself for it.

She should be ecstatic that Jed had made a decision to stay around for Toby. She should be doing cartwheels.

Then why couldn't she shake the feeling that something wasn't quite right, that this façade of familial happiness would come crashing down around her ears at any second?

Toby rolled his eyes. 'I know. I meant on the weekends and after school.'

'Good,' she said, shoving the food around her plate now that she'd lost her appetite.

Thankfully, Jed sensed her discomfort and kept conversation with Toby at a cracking pace, where she only had to offer the occasional 'uh-huh'. Though the more the boys chatted, the more she silently fumed. Sure, she was mad at Jed for not speaking to her before Toby about his future but, if she was completely honest, there was more to it.

It hit her like a bolt of electricity.

She was jealous.

Plain, old-fashioned jealousy that Jed could come into their lives over the last few months and make himself so comfortable that Toby responded to him as if he'd had a dad around his whole life.

'Ready for dessert?' She all but leapt up from

her chair, staggered by the truth and not ready to accept it yet.

She loved Jed. She was jealous of Jed.

Was there any end to the revelations her psyche would spring on her? Maybe she should just have it out with him once and for all and be done with it.

'Mum's made a really cool apple crumble. It's yummy,' Toby said, hastily clearing the plates from the table to make room for his favourite dessert.

'Sounds good.' Jed joined her at the stove, where she was practically throwing huge scoops of crumble into bowls in her haste to get this meal over with.

'You OK?' he said, dropping his voice low as he spooned ice cream over the steaming crumble.

'I've been better,' she snapped, sending him another furious glare before returning to the table with the pudding.

If he'd thought she was in a strange mood before, he would be spinning out at her behaviour now. But she couldn't help it. She was done playing happy families.

Time to set some boundaries. Time to work out where Jed fitted into *their* family, hers and Toby's. The sooner the better.

'Mmm…that was great, Mum. May I be excused? I want to finish off that superhero book Dad got me before bed.'

'Sure, Tobes.' She smiled at her son, determined to do this for him. 'I'll be up later to tuck you in, OK?'

Toby paused at the doorway. 'You too, Dad?'

Jed fired an uncertain glance her way before nodding. 'You bet.'

'Cool!'

They listened to Toby's footsteps clattering up the stairs, dread churning with determination in Aimee's gut.

'Nice of you to tell me your plans.' She launched into him as soon as she heard Toby's bedroom door close, knowing it was now or never.

He shrugged, looking annoyingly casual for a guy about to get a tongue-lashing. 'Toby asked me a direct question about my plans earlier today; I gave him a straight answer.'

'So you're staying?'

'I've decided to move to Melbourne, yes.'

'And you were going to tell me…when?'

'Stop being so territorial.' Jed stood up and cleared the dessert bowls in record time, turning his back on her to stack the dishwasher.

Stupidly, it was the sight of him involved in such a domestic chore, in *her* kitchen, that riled her more than his words.

'What?'

He shook his head, straightened and turned back to face her. 'You're acting like you own Toby and you don't. He's my son too and now that we're getting along you don't like it.'

'That's rubbish,' she said, fighting a rising blush and losing. 'What I don't like is you getting his hopes up and dashing them like you did—'

'With you?'

Two words, soft, cold, lethal.

He sent her a pitying stare before crossing the kitchen to stand less than two feet in front of her.

Cursing that she'd said too much, she tilted her chin up, determined to look him in the eye.

'You need to let go of the past if there's to be any future for us,' he said, reaching out to cup her cheek before she could move.

'Easy for you to say.'

She tried to muster a haughty glare but failed miserably, considering the warmth from his hand seemed to be branding her skin with its heat.

'All I'm asking for is a chance, Aimee. A chance to prove myself. A chance to explain. A chance for us to have a future together. You and me. And Toby.'

His thumb brushed her lips, dwelling on the bottom lip she knew was a hair's breadth away from trembling if he didn't let go.

Could she take a risk and give Jed a second chance? Did she want to?

Loving him was one thing. Dealing with the

consequences if he walked out a second time would be too much.

She didn't know how long they stood there, his steady caramel gaze locked on her nervous hazel one, his hand conveying a reassurance she could scarcely believe, but suddenly the deadlock was shattered by his mobile.

Fishing it from his pocket, he turned away to answer it but not before she'd seen the guilt streak across his face as he checked the call display.

The call was brief, perfunctory and reeked of a subterfuge she'd seen once too often.

His 'yeah's, 'uh-huh's and 'no's didn't tell her a thing. Oh, yes, she'd definitely been down this track before and it scared her to death.

However, he'd asked for a second chance. Time for her to give him a little leeway and see if, this time, things would be different.

'Important call?'

He snapped the mobile shut, slid it into his pocket and pulled out his keys. 'Actually, yes. I have to go.'

'Where?'

Her heart hammered as she gripped the back of a chair for support, *déjà vu* washing over her in sickening waves, nausea churning her stomach. This couldn't be happening...

'Brisbane, then Sydney. I shouldn't be gone more than a few days.'

'What about Toby?'

Pain warred with the guilt on his face. At least he felt more for his son than he had for her, she'd give him that much. When she'd asked the 'where?' question five years ago, he hadn't given her an answer.

'I'll nip up and say goodbye now but I really have to leave.'

'Business?' She kept pushing; she had to. Anything to stop the tidal wave of doubts that threatened to swamp her, to leave her a drowned wreck as it had in the past.

'Sort of.'

Ah...the old evasive flick of the eyes, the not-quite-meeting-her-stare trick. God, she hated that.

'Who are you meeting?'

She hated sounding like this, like a suspicious harpy haranguing her man, but she needed to do this. She needed answers, and this time she'd settle for nothing less.

'Aimee, you have to trust me on this.'

'No!'

She shut her eyes for a second and took a deep breath, trying to stay calm long enough to say what had to be said, before opening them and pinning him with a glare that meant business.

'You want me to *trust* you? Are you kidding? I trusted you in the past and look where that got me.'

She held tight to the back of the chair, needing something as mundane as the familiarity of her old wooden dining chair to steady her before the maelstrom of her emotions swung her out of control.

'I can't talk about this right now.' Jed shook his head, unable to meet her eyes. 'I have to go.'

'Same old, same old,' she said, her voice

dripping with sarcasm as the pain she'd bottled for so long bubbled to the surface in a devastating explosion. 'You don't *have* to do anything! Apart from tell me what the heck is going on.'

He raised stricken eyes to her, his hurt mirroring her own. 'I can't.'

'This is a joke!' She pushed the chair away and spun around, unable to face his pain when he had no right to feel any.

She was the one who was falling apart inside, the one who'd been stupid enough to take the same destructive path again in falling in love with a guy she could never trust.

Clenching her hands, she pressed them against her eyes, warding off the angry tears that stung. She wouldn't cry. He wasn't worth her tears.

Taking several gulps of air, she swung back to face him. 'You know why this is a joke? Because you're the one who's been going on and on about how much you want to be part of this family, about how much Toby means to you, about sticking around forever. Yet when it comes to opening up, to trusting someone, a perfectly normal, healthy part of any family, you can't do it. You're a fraud, Jed. You're still the same guy who couldn't handle commitment five years ago. What makes you think you have what it takes now to handle being part of a family?'

He paled, his tanned face leeched of all colour as he took a step towards her. 'I will explain—'

'No, you won't!' She held up a hand to ward him off but he kept coming anyway.

'You're wrong about me. And I'll prove it to you.'

Before she could react he dropped a soft kiss on her lips, rubbed her arm for an instant and took off up the stairs.

Aimee's legs finally gave out and she sank into the nearest chair and stared out the window, finding little comfort in the city skyline that usually captivated her.

She didn't want his proof. She had all the proof she needed: the phone call, the evasiveness and the lies, just like old times.

Jed wanted a second chance?

Not if he came crawling on his knees and begged her.

CHAPTER FOURTEEN

'THIS is some set-up you've got, Jed, my boy.'

Jed followed his dad into the apartment he'd rented for him near the restaurant, hoping he wasn't making a huge mistake.

'And that restaurant of yours. Talk about fancy!' His dad settled into an armchair by the window and leaned back, hands behind head and feet on the coffee-table as if he'd lived here for years. 'You sure you want riff-raff like me working there?'

'Cut the martyr act. You'll earn your pay like everyone else there.'

Jed wandered aimlessly around the apartment, torn between guilt of abandoning his dad and desperation to head back to Melbourne as soon as possible and finish what he'd started with Aimee before his dad's call.

'Jed?'

The uncertainty in his dad's gruff voice stopped him dead in his tracks. Larry Sanderson was cocky, brash, with the gift of the gab that had got him into trouble more often than not. He never sounded weary or vulnerable, the way he did right now.

'Yeah?'

'I wanted to say thanks for everything you've done. I know I've been a lousy dad yet you've stuck by me, even through the rough times.'

Jed looked at his dad, really looked at him for the first time in years, noting the receding hairline, the grey tufts of hair sprouting from his ears, the roadmap of wrinkles surrounding his coal-black eyes and the sardonic twist of his mouth. His dad looked old, fatigued, as if he'd seen too much and done too much.

No doubt about it, Larry had a lot to answer for, yet for all the dumb things he'd done, for all the hurt he'd inflicted, particularly on his sons, Jed couldn't help but love him.

'What I want to know is why.'

'Why do you think, Dad?'

Confusion clouded his dad's eyes, as if he hadn't understood the question, before his gaze darted around the room as if searching for a way out.

'If your mother had been around, things would've been different,' Larry said, his voice barely perceptible. 'We would've been a family. A real family.'

Jed wouldn't give him an argument there. He'd seen first-hand what having a mother and a father could do for a kid, as Toby had blossomed over the last few months.

'You had a family. Bud, me and you. Don't go making excuses because you mucked up.'

Larry opened his mouth, always quick off the mark with an excuse, before clamping it shut again and shuffling across to the window to stare outside.

'I did muck up, big time. Guess I can never change that.' Once again, regret tinged his father's voice, giving Jed some hope that the old guy could change for the better.

'No, but you can make damn sure you don't repeat the same mistakes.'

A motto he had full intention of living up to with Toby. So raising Bud hadn't worked out? That didn't mean he'd fail again. He'd make sure of it.

'I won't.'

Larry turned back to face him, shoulders slumped, hands in pockets, looking like a defeated man rather than someone who'd left hell behind and had a second chance on life. 'You ever hear from Bud?'

'No.'

He'd tried to contact his brother several times when he'd first heard he'd gone to prison, but Bud had made it clear he wanted no familial visits during his jail time. Jed had lost sleep over that, wondering where he'd gone so wrong that his little brother didn't even want to see him any more.

They'd been so close as teenagers and Jed had done his best to steer the kid right. Obviously, his best hadn't been good enough.

'I'm not surprised.' Larry plopped down into the armchair again, looking a lot less cocky now.

'What's that supposed to mean?'

Dread turned Jed to stone. Did he really want to hear what his dad had to say? Didn't he live with enough guilt every day that he hadn't done enough with Bud?

'Bud and I met about a year ago. Inter-prison work gang, fixing up a road outside of Brisbane. We got to talking.'

Oh, yeah, Jed could hear it coming.

You didn't do enough. You didn't look after your brother like I asked to you. You could've stopped him from stealing that car, from killing that cyclist. Words he'd heard a thousand times before in his own mind.

'Yeah?'

Jed blanked his expression and kept his voice devoid of emotion. He didn't want his dad to see how bad he felt, how guilty he felt for making a hash of being Bud's guardian.

Larry sighed and rubbed a hand over his balding pate. 'Bud was real sorry for letting you down. He said you'd come to visit him a few times but he couldn't face you for the guilt.'

Huh?

What did Bud have to be guilty about? He wasn't the one who'd tried everything to make his little brother listen: Jed had tried being a mate, tried being a father and brother rolled into one, and when that hadn't worked he'd been the forceful guardian, ruling with an iron fist.

Nothing had worked and Bud had gone careening off the rails faster than a runaway train, causing just as much devastation.

'Bud idolised you. Said he wanted to be just like you but he didn't know how. You had clear goals of what you wanted to do with your life;

Bud just wanted to hang out. He hated school, hated being a disappointment to you. That's why he couldn't meet you face to face. He didn't want to see the disappointment in your eyes that he'd let you down. He said you were a great stand-in dad, the best he could've had.'

Jed stared at his father in horror. Was the old man spinning another of his yarns or was this the truth?

Doubt must have shown on his face because Larry leaned over and laid a hand on his arm for the first time in years.

'You did good, son. Real good. A much better father than I could've been to the boy. What happened was an accident, one of those twists of fate that screws up a man's life. Me, I made lousy decisions to screw up mine but Bud is made of better stuff than me. He's more like you. Clever, ambitious, wants to make something of himself once he comes out.'

Jed's heart pounded as the burden he'd carried around for so many years struggled to roll away. His dad sounded genuine but why hadn't Bud ever told him any of this himself? Had he been that unapproachable?

Larry patted his arm and sat back, a serene expression replacing the anxious one of a few moments ago. 'Why do you think I'm out earlier than expected? It's about time I showed you two that old Larry isn't a loser, and thankfully the parole board agreed that my good behaviour wasn't a sham but the real thing. You've made good, Bud's going to make good—what excuse do I have? I've wasted too many years of my life and it's time I started living, as of now. So, why don't we have a beer to celebrate and you can fill me in on what's going on with you?'

As Jed tried to make sense of the information just dumped on him and headed for the fridge, the guilt he'd been carrying like a boulder for so many years rolled off his shoulders and crumbled into pebbles, easy to kick away.

He hadn't screwed up with Bud. His brother

had made a mistake, had learned from it and didn't blame him. Even more unlikely, it looked as if his dad had finally decided to join the real world, a world not consisting of scams and criminals, a world he actually wanted to contribute to. Wonders would never cease.

Grabbing two beers, he strolled back into the lounge and handed one to his dad, unable to keep a growing grin from his face.

He *would* be a good father for Toby.

He wouldn't screw it up.

Yes, there would be tough times ahead, times when he wouldn't have a clue, but then didn't all parents go through that? Besides, he'd have Aimee beside him, supporting him, and that was all a guy could ask for.

'Here's to dads and their sons.'

Jed tapped his bottle against his dad's, Larry's answering smile filled with pride all the encouragement he needed to sit down and get him up to speed with his plans.

* * *

Aimee stabbed the knife into a perfectly formed mango cheesecake, hacking it into rough pieces when the delicious dessert deserved better treatment. Then again, Marsha's book club had never complained before and she doubted they'd notice a few rough-around-the-edges bits.

She'd been like this ever since Jed had run out on them two nights ago: uninterested, unmotivated and totally spun out. Baking had proved her solace on so many occasions before, especially when he'd broken her heart first time around, but this time the hurt went deeper.

Jed wasn't stupid. Yes, she'd refused his proposal and yes, she'd tried to re-establish a friendship between them for Toby's sake, but he'd seen right through her, culminating in that heart-rending moment in her kitchen, where for one second she'd allowed herself to dream. To embrace the possibility of what could happen if she gave them the second chance he'd asked for.

Before reality had intruded, she'd asked the hard questions and he'd fobbed her off. Just for old times' sake.

What sort of a guy did that? Play on a person's emotions when they had no intention of following through? When they had the same old secrets, the same old baggage they wouldn't unlock even if the chance they'd just asked for depended on it?

A stupid guy, and, as much as she'd like to shut Jed completely out of her life for good, she couldn't. Toby loved his dad, the only reason she'd agreed to meeting him here today.

She hadn't answered his calls yesterday, deleting each and every one with a vicious stab at the answering machine and her mobile. Finally, after hearing the genuine worry in his voice when he thought Toby had taken a turn for the worse, she'd sent him a brief text message, saying Toby was OK and she'd be around the shop today at six if he wanted to talk.

Correction. If she talked and he listened. The

emotional merry-go-round had to stop, right here, right now, and she intended on making it clear that the subject of second chances and other such nonsense wasn't open for discussion.

She'd sent Toby on a short walk with Marsha, not prepared to give Jed more than ten minutes of her time. Their meeting had to focus on Toby. If it veered on to the delicate subject of their parting, she'd cut him off just as she'd cut a nougat slice into bite-size pieces a few minutes ago: quick, sharp, brutal.

Glancing out the window, she caught sight of Jed striding along Acland St, his confident steps eating up the pavement, a man with places to go, things to do, in total contrast to the old man beside him, practically running to keep up.

Jed had things to do all right, to make her life a living hell, and she wouldn't make it easy for him.

But what was with the old guy? He didn't look like a mate of a go-getter like Jed, in his worn camel corduroys and plaid shirt, a bemused expression on his face as if he expected a genie to pop out and grant him a wish any second. He had a vaguely familiar air, though she couldn't place him. Might be one of Jed's old chef buddies, but what was he doing bringing him to meet her at a time like this?

Wiping her hands, she whipped her apron over her head, took a quick glance in the mirror to make sure she didn't look as frazzled as she felt and took several deep breaths, eager to get this over and done with. The sooner she established Jed's boundaries with Toby, the sooner she wouldn't have to see him again.

She'd already worked out that Marsha could handle the access visits, leaving her to mend her broken heart in peace. Again.

Sheesh! Would she never learn?

'Hi, Aimee. How are you?'

Jed wandered into the shop, his spicy aftershave mingling with the cinnamon and nutmeg fragrance hanging in the air, creating an all-too-delicious combination, while his friend waited outside, looking as nervous as she felt.

'Fine.' She kept her response brief, clipped, impersonal, the exact way she planned on talking to him for the duration of this inevitable meeting.

Jed smiled, a tight, anxious, upward-tilting of his lips, the complete antithesis of his usual confidence. 'Hope you don't mind but I've brought someone to meet you.'

'This isn't really the time for a social visit, surely?'

She glanced at the old man, who had his face almost pressed against the glass pane, staring at her cake display like a kid ogling the latest computer-game release. There was something about him...

'Listen, I know I didn't have a chance to finish what I started to say the other night or to explain half the things I wanted to. I hoped I could try again today.'

Aimee's heart gave a familiar flutter at the

imploring look in his golden eyes before she remembered the hurt, the all-consuming pain of loving a guy like Jed and being let down by him. Repeatedly.

'I'm not interested in rehashing anything,' she said, turning away and nibbling on a fingernail while furiously marshalling her defences.

Why was he doing this? Didn't he get the message from her terse text message, from the unanswered calls? If not, she would have thought her frosty welcome might have given him a clue as to how downright furious she was with him for hurting her again, yet here he was, ready to prolong the whole disaster?

Not if she could help it.

'Just get to the point, Jed. Toby and Marsha will be back shortly and I want this settled before then.'

Jed pinned her with a determined look that would have impressed her if she hadn't been immune to whatever he had to say.

'I owe you the truth.'

'You owe me nothing,' she said, ignoring the niggle of curiosity that made her search his face for some sign of his intentions.

Was he toying with her or had he actually grown a conscience at this late stage?

'Yes, I do. I need you to give me a chance to explain.'

By the slight raising of his voice, she could have assumed he was desperate. Or playing her again.

'I don't want to hear your explanations. Don't you see? Nothing you say will make a difference.'

Saying the words, she felt better, stronger, a woman trying to stand by her convictions. Before she fell apart completely.

'That's my father out there.'

Her head snapped up, swivelling between the old man outside and the man she loved, the man she thought she'd once known better than herself, the man who'd once told her his father was dead and he had no family.

'*What?*'

'I lied to you.' He ran a hand through his hair, his weary expression ageing him before her eyes. 'Though I guess you've already figured out that part. My dad's alive and he's the reason I left you five years ago.'

'This is insane,' she muttered, gripping on to the marble counter and blinking rapidly to dispel the spots before her eyes.

He had hold of her arm before she could steady herself and led her to a chair. 'You need to sit down.'

'What I need is to get my ears cleaned. I could've sworn you just said that old man is your dad and he's the reason you bailed out on us.'

She shook her head, trying to make sense of what she'd just heard but coming up empty. Not only had Jed held secrets, run out on her and broken her heart, but she could now also add liar to the illustrious list.

'I know this explanation comes years too late, but if you'll hear me out I'm hoping you'll understand.' He squatted next to her and took hold of her hand. She stared down at his large, tanned hand holding her small pale one, knowing this was beyond crazy but suddenly needing to hear what he had to say.

She'd wanted closure today, right? Well, it looked as if her wish was about to come true, in spades.

'None of this makes sense. Why would you lie to me about not having any family?'

'Because I was ashamed,' he said, pulling up a chair next to her and sliding into it without letting go of her hand. She could have snatched it out of his grip but, right now, she was willing to take what little comfort she could get. By the time she'd heard Jed out, she had a feeling she'd need it.

'Ashamed of your father? But that's ridiculous!'

She'd loved her dad unconditionally and there wasn't a day that went by when she didn't miss him. He'd been the one man she could depend on in this world, the one man who had never let her down.

'Five years ago, my dad was involved in a major armed robbery. It was all over the Press, front-page news, and I knew once his trial started up it could get ugly.'

A light bulb switched on in her head at the time factor. 'That spate of phone calls, your secret absences. Was that about your dad?'

He nodded, a flicker of relief flashing in his eyes that she understood. 'I wanted to tell you but I couldn't. You were always talking about your perfect family, especially your dad, and I didn't want you embroiled in my mess.'

'But we were living together. We shared everything; we loved each other…' She trailed off, saddened that Jed hadn't thought enough of their relationship to confide in her.

'And I didn't want to risk tainting that love with an ugly, drawn-out court battle where the media could've dragged you through the mud. Your family business here was famous—I couldn't jeopardise that. You would've ended up hating me for it.'

'Instead of hating you for ruining what we had by running away?'

He shrugged, flinching slightly at her words. 'Guess I hoped that, once the trial was over, we might have a chance to pick up where we left off. However, once I got back to Dunk Island, you'd left for Melbourne. I tried calling and writing but you didn't want a bar of me so I gave up. I'd made my choice and, in sticking by my dad, I lost you and I've blamed him every day since.'

Aimee glanced outside at Jed's father, who had given up drooling over her cake display and had taken a seat on a wooden bench, content to watch the world go by. What seemed vaguely familiar before crystallised into startling clarity: the two men had the same firm jaw, the slightly prominent nose, the impressive cheekbones. However, Jed's father bore a weatherbeaten expression that said he'd seen the rougher side of life and had survived.

'This is some story,' she said, quickly looking away as Jed's dad glanced up and locked gazes with her.

'Ah, but there's more.' Jed squeezed her hand, his grip imploring her to listen just a little longer.

'I have a brother too, Bud.'

'Well, well, well. Just one big happy family,' she said, wondering if anything he'd ever told her had been the truth.

Had their entire relationship back then been a sham? Had he really loved her as he'd professed so many times?

He sighed, rubbing his eyes as if to erase painful memories. 'I practically raised Bud. Dad was always involved in crooked schemes that landed him in trouble so he'd have to disappear for long stretches at a time, or several bigger schemes that landed him in jail a few times. Bud was a good kid and I wanted the best for him. I tried my best to be the father dad couldn't be for either of us but it wasn't enough. Bud soon started doing stupid stuff like breaking into cars, fooling around with the wrong crowd. I tried to pull him back but the harder I tried, the more he rebelled. Then he killed someone.'

'Oh, my God.' Aimee clasped Jed's hand between both of hers, raising it to her lips before she knew what she was doing. Her first instinct was to comfort the man whose family was the antithesis of hers and then some.

'Bud stole a car, went for a joyride and killed a cyclist. Accidentally, of course, but he was speeding, he'd just turned eighteen, so they threw the book at him. He's still inside.'

Pain turned Jed's eyes a deep topaz and she wanted to pull him into her arms and cradle him close, despite her own hurt at how he'd treated her.

She searched for something to say, anything to break the awkward silence. What did he expect of her? Did he want her sympathy? Did he expect this to change anything between them? Because it didn't.

Yes, she understood family loyalty but Jed hadn't trusted her enough to explain all this years ago.

Yes, she respected the fact he hadn't wanted to embroil her or her family in a possible scandal but he could have explained the facts to her before walking out.

She could understand all these things but what she didn't get was why any of this should have made a difference. They'd been invincible back then; they could have taken on the world together if only he'd loved her enough to keep the faith.

But he hadn't. He'd made a choice, a choice that had cost them a chance at being a real family: her, Jed and Toby.

'I'm sorry,' she said, knowing it sounded inadequate but incapable of saying anything more. Besides, what could she say? That he'd tossed away their future without trusting her enough to be a part of that decision?

'No, I'm the one who's sorry. I loved you so much but I had no idea how to handle it. Sure,

lots of kids blame their bad decisions on dysfunctional upbringings but I honestly didn't
know how you'd react if I told you the truth.
Trust wasn't big in my family when I was
growing up and every person I trusted let me
down. I just couldn't bear that coming from
you too, so I walked away before things got too
complicated.'

She wanted to yell 'But they already were too
complicated! We made a baby together.'
However, his soft words combined with his
genuine sadness touched her like nothing he'd
said to date.

It was easy for her to sit here and judge him.
She'd had the perfect family, their constant love
and support, and she had trusted her parents
with her life.

When she'd returned home pregnant and devastated at losing the love of her life, they hadn't
asked questions. They hadn't berated her or
chastised her or made her feel like a fool.
Instead, they'd opened their arms and com-

forted her, supporting her every step of the way through her pregnancy and beyond. She'd been blessed, while Jed had struggled in a role most young men wouldn't even dream of taking on, let alone making a go of it.

Of course his bad family experience would taint his view of relationships, would shatter his ability to trust. And she'd shoved those trust issues down his throat the last time they had met.

'I think I understand,' she said, the first stirrings of hope pulling against the tight, defensive bind around her heart.

If Jed came clean about everything, maybe they had a chance at a future after all?

'I loved you so much' was what he'd just said. *Loved*, as in past tense, and just like that her hope dwindled and faded to nothing.

'I'd hoped you would.' He clasped her hand tighter while she yearned to yank it out of his grip, needing space to get through what would be a final farewell as she'd expected before this meeting started.

'That call two nights ago when I ran out of here?'

She nodded, the bitterness flooding back as she thought history was repeating itself.

'My dad got released from prison early. I had to be there to pick him up. I'd arranged an apartment for him in Sydney and a job at my restaurant up there and I needed to make sure he got settled. I was afraid he might slip up if I left him to his own devices even for a day, so I ran.' He paused, his steady stare compelling her to look at him, the intensity behind his stare scaring her. 'I've done a lot of running from you in the past but I promise you this: I will never run from you or Toby again. You're my family now. You come first and always will. My dad and I have sorted through a lot of emotional stuff and I've shed my hang-ups about not being a good enough dad. I'm here for the long haul. You *can* trust me.'

Tears sprang to her eyes and she blinked them away, wishing he'd stop staring at her as if she was his world. She wasn't and she could never give him what he wanted, no matter how many pretty speeches he made.

'I can't be part of the family you want,' she said, wrenching her hand free and springing up from the chair. 'Toby is your son and I think you'll be a great dad for him. But as for being a family, I can't fill the void for you and I won't put Toby through some sham that everything is great between his parents when it's not.' She dabbed at her cheeks, a futile gesture at trying to stem the tears that had turned into a mini-flood.

Jed stood and calmly approached her, taking small steps and holding out his hand as if to reassure a wild animal.

'I don't need a void filled. I need you. I've always needed you. You're the only woman I've ever loved. The only woman I want to spend the rest of my life with. As much as I love Toby, even if the little guy wasn't around, I would still love you with all my heart.'

She stared at him, hearing the words but having

a hard time processing them as her mind whirled with the implication of what he was saying, and he took advantage of her pause to continue.

'When you first summoned me to Melbourne, I hoped we could rekindle the magic we once had but then I learned about Toby and I was so damn angry with you I couldn't think straight. It took me a while to accept what you were telling me let alone jump feet first into a father role I'd always thought I was lousy at. I thought I would never forgive you but then I started thinking and feeling and, once I got a handle on the giant chip on my shoulder and realised how much I still loved you, I knew that I had to let it all go. All of it, the anger, the resentment, the shame of my family, all of it, and take a chance that you'd still love me too.'

Jed loved her.

Jed *loved* her!

Her feet flew towards him, closing the short gap between them in an instant and she flung herself into his arms, sobbing her heart out.

'Though you threw the ring back at me during my proposal a while back, I'm hoping this means you do still have a soft spot for me?' he murmured, smoothing her hair, cuddling her close, his body warmth infusing her right down to her soul and dispelling the last of the icy despair that lingered from the past.

'I threw that ring at you because I thought you didn't love me as much as I love you, you big dope!' She lifted her head from his shoulder and smiled up at him, his familiar features blurred through her tears. The features she would spend the rest of her life waking up next to, touching, kissing, loving.

'Yeah, that wasn't the world's greatest proposal, was it?' He smiled, running a finger down her nose, tracing her lips, feathering across her skin till she tingled.

'Think you can do better?' She quirked an eyebrow at him, reverting to the bold, sassy woman she'd once been, the woman he'd loved.

'I know I can. But right now we have an

audience, so I think I'll save it for later.' He took hold of her shoulders and gently turned her around to look out the window, where Jed's father, Toby and Marsha all had their faces pressed against the glass.

Aimee laughed, rested her head on Jed's shoulder and beckoned them in.

Toby raced in first and came to a skidding halt in front of them. 'So, did she say yes, Dad? Did she like the ring? Are we going to live together and be the family we talked about?'

Aimee's mouth dropped as she fixed Jed with an 'explain this one, mister' look.

Jed merely grinned and bent down to hoist Toby onto his shoulders, placing a secure arm around her waist once he'd straightened. 'Toby and I had a man-to-man talk the other day. I told him how much I love his mum and how much I love him.'

'I even got to see the ring, Mum. Isn't it cool?' Toby patted her head from his perch, the mirror image of his supremely confident father now that she'd told him how she really felt.

'Very cool,' she said, the irony that her son had known before she had that Jed loved her not lost.

He'd spoken the truth. He did love her, had told Toby about it beforehand, yet she'd doubted him. Not any more.

'And this old man knows Dad.' Toby pointed at Jed's father, who stepped forward with a sheepish grin on his face.

'Toby!' Aimee said, wondering how to approach a one-time felon before dismissing her fears as ridiculous. This man was Jed's father and if he'd come to terms with his past, so could she.

'Hi, I'm Aimee. Pleased to meet you.' She offered her hand to Jed's father, wishing she knew his name.

'Larry Sanderson. Very pleased to meet you.' His callused handshake was firm, confident, while his black eyes twinkled at her. 'My son's spoken a lot about you and I can see why he loves you so much.'

'Thanks.' Aimee blushed, heat flooding her cheeks as she searched for something to say.

Once again, Toby came to the rescue. 'Did you just say my dad is your son?'

Larry nodded, his gaze fixed on Toby. 'That's right. Do you know what that makes me?'

Toby nodded, suddenly shy, his eyes growing to saucer-like proportions.

'I'm your grandpa. Is that OK with you?'

Aimee held her breath. Toby had had a lot to cope with the past year and this sudden intro-duction only added to it.

Toby screwed up his eyes as if thinking, before sitting up straighter with a wide grin on his face. 'I had a grandpa but he died. I guess it would be cool to have another one.'

'That's good,' Larry said, holding out his hand to Toby, who shook it with great solemnity.

Aimee shot a glance at Jed, whose grin rivalled Toby's and Larry's, and the last of her doubts faded.

They were a family now.

Sure, families trusted, supported and encour-aged each other but they also squabbled, argued and went through rough patches. No doubt, her new family would be no different and they'd get through it. She had no doubt because they had a lot more than most families and that was love.

'How about we all have some afternoon tea? You too, Marsha,' Aimee said as she spied her nanny-cum-manager trying to slip out the door.

'Brilliant idea.' Larry beamed like a man who'd been given the world on a platter. 'Aimee, if those cakes taste half as good as they look, you might find a permanent customer camped on your doorstep.'

'They're really yummy, Grandpa. Just wait till you try one!' Toby slithered to the ground as Jed bent down, his hand snaking out to capture hers before she headed for the counter.

'About that proposal…' he whispered in her ear, placing a soft kiss on the tender skin beneath and eliciting a whole host of responses, none of which were appropriate for this gathering.

Aimee chuckled, kissing Jed on the mouth before pulling away. 'Later, my darling. Can't you see we've got family to take care of?'

EPILOGUE

'YOU ready to get this show on the road?'

Aimee took a deep breath and placed her hand on Larry's proffered arm, wishing her quaking belly would stop. After all, what did she have to be nervous about? She'd never been surer of anything in her life.

'Ready,' she said, smiling at the man she'd got to know and like over the last month. 'What about you? You look ready to pass out.'

'Not before I get you married off to my son.' He winked and placed a kiss on her cheek. 'You're an amazing woman, Aimee Payet, and Jed is lucky to have you. Make sure you remind him of that every day.'

'I will.'

She laughed, a nervous giggle bordering on

hysteria, and Larry must've picked up on it, as he placed a hand firmly on hers and turned her towards the stretch of sand they had to negotiate before reaching her destiny.

Larry hummed a jaunty tune under his breath as they fell into step, Aimee's concentration fixed on the tableau standing near the water's edge on St Kilda beach.

She'd had her magical proposal when Jed had taken her on a hot-air balloon ride high above Melbourne, plying her with champagne and words of love as he tried a second time with the exquisite ring, which she allowed to be firmly placed on her third finger. As they'd drifted along he'd pointed out the Rialto, where his newest restaurant was soon to open, making sure she'd agreed to supply the pastries before telling the balloon pilot to head back to earth.

So her fiancé was into bribery? If it was his only vice, she could live with it. Besides, his convincing techniques were sensational!

A harpist played a soft melody as Aimee and Larry reached the small group gathered on the sand. She would have recognised the song if she'd been concentrating. As it was, she only had eyes for Jed, looking resplendent in a casual beige suit with an open-necked white shirt accentuating his tan.

'Mum, you look like a princess!' Toby yelled out, bouncing up and down next to Jed, decked out in a miniature outfit the same as his father's, cuter and cheekier than ever, while Marsha gave her a thumbs-up sign of approval next to the minister.

'Show time,' Larry said, placing her hand gently in Jed's, stopping briefly to pat Jed on the back and sending her a reassuring wink before taking his place alongside his son.

'You're exquisite,' Jed said, placing a lingering kiss against her lips, a kiss full of promise, a forever kind of kiss, before pulling back to let his admiring gaze roam her simple ivory sheath.

'And you're my type of guy,' she said, squeezing his hand and turning to face the minister as proceedings got underway.

The service was short and sweet, just the way they'd wanted it, and before she knew what was happening Jed had kissed her senseless to the rousing applause of Toby, Larry and Marsha and the small wedding party had convened to a private room at the nearby Prince of Wales Hotel for a celebration.

A celebration that would continue well into the night as Aimee and Jed set about reaffirming their love, many times, intimately.

However, before the bride and groom slipped away, Toby had one more job to do.

'Mum, Dad. I know it's Christmas next week and I've asked for loads of presents but I think not having to see the doctor any more because I'm all better and getting a dad and a grandpa is the best present ever.'

He paused and widened his eyes for full effect. He'd learned that every time he made this face, his mum got a gooey look in her eyes and his dad grinned.

'But I think I'd still like the presents too!'

'We'll see what Santa brings you,' his mum said, hugging him close and smothering him in that smelly stuff she wore whenever his dad was around, while his dad ruffled his hair, something he'd grown to like, seeing as it made his dad happy. He could tell his dad was happy by the way those wrinkly lines around his eyes creased up.

'Don't you have something to give your mum, champ?'

'Oh, yeah.'

Toby fished around in his pocket, hoping he hadn't lost the box. His dad had given it to him five minutes ago and told him to be very careful, but since then he'd found a really long streamer, a coin and a popper thingy that he'd stuffed in there too.

As his fingers closed around the hard square

box he pulled it out, snagging it on his pocket and hearing a small ripping sound. 'Bugger!'

'Toby!' His mum stared at him, that awful frown in the middle of her forehead, the kind she got when he'd done something wrong.

'Grandpa says it,' he said, blurting out the first thing that came to his mind, knowing it wasn't a good move when a matching frown appeared on his dad's forehead.

'You shouldn't repeat everything you hear grown-ups say, son,' his dad said, his frown disappearing as he caught sight of the box Toby held out.

'That's right,' his mum said, shaking her head, making her curly hair tickle his face as she leaned down to look at the box. 'What's that?'

'A surprise from Dad and me,' he said, hoping she liked it and hoping it wiped that nasty frown off her forehead even more.

His mum was always doing nice stuff for him, like making his lunches and bringing him surprises to cheer him up when he'd been ill. In fact, even now that he was all better, she did fun things with him and he wanted to do something nice for her. His dad had agreed. In fact, his dad had hugged him really tight when he'd come up with the idea.

'Go on, open it, Mum. You'll like it.'

His mum opened the box really slowly, like grown-ups did. If it were him, he would've ripped it open really quickly.

'Oh!' Her hand covered her mouth as she looked at him and his dad, her eyes getting that funny watery look that signalled tears.

Yuck, he hated tears.

'Isn't it the coolest? When I saw Dad had half of that circle thing on a bit of chain in his wallet, I remembered you had a circle thingy too, in your jewellery box. So I asked Dad if we could put the two together and make a whole one and give it to you for a present.'

'It's beautiful,' his mum said, swooping down and giving him the biggest hug ever, before giving his dad a big, mushy kiss on the lips and hugging him too.

'You kept it all these years,' his dad said, staring at his mum with that goo-goo look they did all the time now.

His mum nodded, slipping the necklace out of the box and clipping it around her neck, alongside the bigger, sparklier necklace she'd worn for the wedding, the one that made her look like a princess.

'And you did too. Looks like the two halves of our yin and yang were always meant to be together,' she said, kissing his dad again.

'Gross!' Toby said, wriggling out of her embrace, ready to go back to his grandpa and have some cake now that he'd done his job.

'We love you, Tobes,' his mum said, blowing him a kiss, while his dad said,

'We love you a lot, champ. A huge lot.'

Toby grinned and skipped away, happier than he'd ever been. He wasn't ill any more, he started school next year and he could start back at little athletics soon.

Having a dad was the coolest, having a family the best.

Now, if only Santa brought him that superhero jigsaw next week, his life would be complete.

MILLS & BOON® PUBLISH EIGHT LARGE PRINT TITLES A MONTH. THESE ARE THE EIGHT TITLES FOR DECEMBER 2006

LOVE-SLAVE TO THE SHEIKH
Miranda Lee

HIS ROYAL LOVE-CHILD
Lucy Monroe

THE RANIERI BRIDE
Michelle Reid

THE ITALIAN'S BLACKMAILED MISTRESS
Jacqueline Baird

HAVING THE FRENCHMAN'S BABY
Rebecca Winters

FOUND: HIS FAMILY
Nicola Marsh

SAYING YES TO THE BOSS
Jackie Braun

COMING HOME TO THE COWBOY
Patricia Thayer

MILLS & BOON®

Live the emotion

1106 Rom